"Kress, a witty and engaging writer, creates chilling suspense as twisty as a DNA double helix."
—*Publishers Weekly*

"It's hard to imagine a better writer of science fiction in America today than Nancy Kress."
—*Salt Lake Tribune*

"Devilishly inventive."
—CNN.com

"A depth of imagination unusual even among science fiction writers."
—*Analog*

"Kress has the magical ability of weaving amazing plot, believable science, and intriguing characters into a coherent whole."
—*Blogcritics*

"Kress combines intriguing scientific speculation with strong human drama to create a finely crafted story."
—*Asimov's Science Fiction*

Praise for the Nebula Award–winning
After the Fall, Before the Fall, During the Fall

"*After the Fall, Before the Fall, During the Fall* is the coming-of-age story for the human race. Nancy Kress has written a chillingly plausible tale of the end of the world."
—Mary Robinette Kowal, author of *The Calculating Stars*

"Nancy Kress displays all her usual strengths in *After the Fall, Before the Fall, During the Fall*: strong plotting, fast-paced action, complex and interesting characters, thought-provoking speculation. But there's something more here: a beautiful meditation on the fate of the earth, an elegy, a warning—and a glimpse of hope."
—Lisa Goldstein, author of *The Red Magician*

"The book is typical Kress, which means impossible to put down."
—Jack McDevitt, author of *Infinity Beach* and *Echo*

"An elegant novella that combines several wildly different science fiction ideas into a tight package. There's a little bit of everything here: time travel, hard science, environmental collapse, aliens, post-apocalyptic dystopia. It may sound hard to combine all of these in such a short format, but Nancy Kress makes it work."
—*Tor.com*

Praise for the Nebula Award–winning *Yesterday's Kin*

"Consider this novella one of the most extreme versions of 'Can women have it all?' in recent fiction, with serious family conflict and alien predators to boot."
—*Glamour*

"Nancy Kress delivers one of the strongest stories of the year to date."
—Gardner Dozois, editor of The Year's Best Science Fiction series

Other books by Nancy Kress

Novels

The Prince of Morning Bells (1981)
The Golden Grove (1984)
The White Pipes (1985)
An Alien Light (1988)
Brain Rose (1990)
Maximum Light (1998)
Nothing Human (2003)
Crossfire (2003)
Crucible (2004)
Dogs (2008)
Steal Across the Sky (2009)
Flash Point (2012)

Sleepless Series

Beggars in Spain (1993)
Beggars and Choosers (1994)
Beggars Ride (1996)

Probability Sun Trilogy

Probability Moon (2000)
Probability Sun (2001)
Probability Space (2002)

Novellas

After the Fall, Before the Fall, During the Fall (2012)
Yesterday's Kin (2014)

Collections

Trinity and Other Stories (1985)
The Aliens of Earth (1993)
Beaker's Dozen (1998)
Nano Comes to Clifford Falls and Other Stories (2008)
AI Bound: Two Stories of Artificial Intelligence (2012)
The Body Human: Three Stories of Future Medicine (2012)
Fountain of Age: Stories (2012)
Future Perfect: Six Stories of Genetic Engineering (2012)
The Best of Nancy Kress (2015)

NANCY KRESS

SEA CHANGE

TACHYON PUBLICATIONS
SAN FRANCISCO

Sea Change
Copyright © 2020 by Nancy Kress

Cover and interior design by Elizabeth Story
Author photo by Liza Trombi

Tachyon Publications LLC
1459 18th Street #139
San Francisco, CA 94107
(415) 285-5615
tachyon@tachyonpublications.com
www.tachyonpublications.com

Series Editor: Jacob Weisman
Project Editor: Jill Roberts

Print ISBN: 978-1-61696-331-6
Digital ISBN: 978-1-61696-332-3

Printed in the United States of America by Versa Press, Inc.

First Edition: 2020

9   8   7   6   5   4   3   2   1

FOR JACK

"One thing is sure: the earth is more cultivated and developed now than ever before; there is more farming and fewer forests, swamps are drying up and cities are springing up on an unprecedented scale. We have become a burden to our planet. Resources are becoming scarce and soon nature will no longer be able to satisfy our needs."

—Quintus Septimius Tertullianus, 200 BCE

THE HOUSE WAS CLEARLY LOST.

I watched from my seat on the second-story balcony of the Cinnamon Café as the tiny house, a ten-by-fifteen imitation Cape Cod with a single dormer, wavered in the middle of the intersection below. It turned to the left, to the right, back to the left, ending up crosswise to the intersection. Traffic honked and stopped. The house didn't budge, probably recalibrating. An ancient Lexus with an ancient driver tried to swerve around the house, but there wasn't enough room. The driver leaned out and shouted at the house—as if that would do any good. Whoever was inside had the shutters closed.

Several homeless, who were not supposed to be in this historic-preservation neighborhood, jeered and laughed.

The robo-server wheeled up to my table. "Can

I bring you something else, ma'am?" I waved it away; my beer was only half drunk. And the show below was too entertaining to gulp the rest, even though I would be late to meet the new recruit. Let him wait. From now on, his life would include a lot of waiting.

The old man in the Lexus, surprisingly spry, jumped out of the car and pounded on the door of the house. Nothing. People in cars, both drivies and manual, leaned out of their windows, looking impatient. One of the homeless threw a plastic cup at the house's back wall. It missed. A few pedestrians stopped to watch, smiling, probably gloating that they weren't the ones whose important rushing was being interrupted by an edifice with confused GPS.

Still the house didn't move. Mobile conveyances this large weren't permitted on city streets unless occupied, although that didn't guarantee that the occupants weren't asleep or drunk or too busy having sex to notice that their dwelling wasn't moving. At the very least, by now the mandatory pull-to-curbside auxiliary engine should have engaged. Somewhere in the distance, a siren sounded, probably cops trying to get through the increasingly snarled traffic.

Grinning, I leaned forward for a better view, and that's when I saw the windowsill below a closed shutter. Simultaneously, my pocket pinged, just once. Not my phone—the D. It only operated at a distance of fewer than twenty-five feet, to avoid electronic surveillance.

I walked down the stairs, forcing myself to not hurry, to look like any other person strolling around Pioneer Square in the rare October sunshine. The ping from my D was significant, but it was the paint on the windowsill that propelled me, a specific and ugly shade called Tiffany Teal. The famous New York jewelry store should have sued over the name. The paint company, after spectacularly bad sales, had discontinued the color. Tiffany Teal was roughly the color of wet cleanser and it went with no other color in the known universe. It was the first thing every new recruit memorized, drilled until they could distinguish it from Azure, Leaf, Evening Sky, and Pale Turquoise. We possessed gallons of it, all that was left in the United States, in multiple discreet locations.

Every organization needs a signature color, Eric Kitson had said, among his other stupid utterances. "Blues" are cops. "Reds" are Communists, unless you live in Boston, where they're a baseball team. "Oranges" are historic Irish enemies. "Pinks" are a girl band. I could go on, but the argument was too dumb, Eric Kitson was dead, and Tiffany Teal paint was used only to signal presence of the Org. It was useful only for line-of-sight, but on the other hand, it couldn't be hacked, unlike all other forms of communication, and the Org knew better than to trust what the government or software companies said about digital security. Not since Kitson's murder.

The house had a single step leading to its single door. The driver who'd pounded on the door had retreated in disgust; he sat in the front seat of his car, shouting into his phone. In one of the backed-up cars, not too far away, a child wailed. Surreptitiously I pinged open the door with my D, turned to give a theatrically amazed look to onlookers, and ducked inside to the blatting of the alarm system. The siren was much closer now. I had only a minute or two.

There was nobody in the tiny house.

It had a loft bed—no time to go up there—a galley kitchen, fold-down table, two easy chairs, bookshelves, a TV. The door to the bathroom was open. I darted in, took the toothbrush, and barely had time to swallow my D. Saliva deactivated its mechanism. The D was soft but nearly a half-inch square, and it got stuck partway down my throat, which gave my voice a strangled gasp when I turned to two cops who filled the doorway.

"The door . . . it was . . . was—" *go down my throat, damn it!* "—open . . . I heard a child—" the D finally finished its trip down my gullet "—crying and I thought someone might need . . ."

I'd always been a more than passable actress. Jake would have been proud of me. Or maybe not, given . . . everything. But I gave the cops the tremulous shakiness of a shy-but-compassionate middle-aged woman trespassing to save a child. I also had: real trepidation creasing my face, a fake ID in my wallet that matched my fake retina scan, and fury in my blood for whatever missing agent of the Org had put me in this position. If it had been an agent. The alternative was worse.

Most of all, I felt fear. Not for myself but for the organization that always hovered between detection and ineptitude, the organization made of dedicated amateurs up against both law-enforcement professionals and a stupid public, the organization that I would protect with everything in the world until we'd succeeded in our quixotic attempt to save that—probably unworthy—world from itself, whether it wanted that or not.

Sometimes the world doesn't know what's best for it.

Only one of the cops, the one in uniform, did the talking. Middle-aged and stocky, he balanced exasperation with boredom; a traffic problem didn't interest him much. It didn't interest the younger one, either, who wore a suit and spent most of his time scrutinizing the inside of the lost house. His silky brown hair wanted cutting; it kept flopping over his eyes in, I assumed, a misguided attempt to look like the pop singer Canton Sparks. Not a chance—his eyes were the same blue but his nose was too big, his lips too thin. Ah, vanity.

They didn't keep me long. "Caroline Denton" did not own a drivie house, had no priors, and possessed ID that matched her retina scan. She had a job with Dugan Brothers Temp Agency. Routine police-wanding showed no electronic devices except a cell phone; by now the D would have dissolved in my stomach acid into its nano-components. But I would have been happier to talk to cops had I not been in my Caroline Denton identity. Much happier.

However, I recorded a witness statement, since abandoning a self-driving house to drive alone was a misdemeanor. Then I left, concealing how shaken I felt.

Who was supposed to have been in the house? And where were they? Arrested, kidnapped, defected?

The problem—one of the problems—with any modern resistance movement is that anything can be hacked. *Anything*—as three presidential elections, the Wall Street Great Meltdown, the Catastrophe, and Kitson's murder all proved. The reconstituted Org takes no chances. None of our communications are electronic. We use couriers like me and, only if we have to, the U.S. mail. We use verbal codes. We use methods that would be familiar during World War II. Except that back then, they had radios and the mechanical Enigma machine. We don't even do that. We rely on our members' brains, also a fallible storage-and-communication system, but at least a hacker in China or at DAS or in one of the fanatical Luddite movements can't obtain documentation of what we're doing.

They can, of course, obtain our brains. Where was the Org agent who should have been in the wandering house?

The new recruit would be waiting for me in Lincoln Park. He'd wait all day and all night if necessary. If he didn't, he was no longer our recruit. I had three choices: leave him there, meet with him first and then go alone to report the wandering house to Kyle, or grab the recruit and take him with me to meet Kyle.

By the time I reached West Seattle, I had decided. I would meet him first. I have good instincts about people.

Lincoln Park in October was lovely. Not New England lovely, where I'd gone to college; the Pacific Northwest ran more to coniferous trees than deciduous. But the park, bordering Puget Sound, had an unusual number of maples and birches, and I crunched through a colorful blanket of leaves on my way to the water. The air smelled earthy, of pine and loam and, somewhere, a hint of mint. People passed me, walking dogs or holding hands, a few children running ahead and shouting. Cops patrolled to keep homeless encampments from forming on park grounds. A peaceful autumnal Eden, just as if the economy had not been nearly destroyed ten years ago and was not still, for the bottom of the human pyramid, an unholy mess.

The recruit sat on the designated park bench facing the bay, exactly where he was supposed to be. I approached him from behind, scrutinizing carefully. He stretched out his arms, probably stiff from the long wait, and I saw the flash of the Tiffany Teal bracelet on his left wrist. "Hello," I said, and he rose and turned toward me.

Sometimes not even superb and relentless training can keep shock from showing on your face, if only for a moment. The recruit registered it, for which I would have given him points if I hadn't, for the second time in two hours, felt so shaken.

He looked like Ian. An Ian who'd been allowed to grow up, who hadn't died during the Catastrophe. Same dark hair curling over his ears, same full lips and gray eyes flecked with gold. After that first shock, the differences became clearer: This kid, at twenty-three, was of course heavier and more muscular than Ian had been at twelve. The recruit's ears stuck out more. But he was a good-looking young man, and I felt a flash of utterly insane pride that my son might have grown up to look like this, might have been the benefit to the world that this recruit, whom I would know as "Tom Fairwood," might be.

Genes, even coincidental genes, are funny things. And it *was* coincidental; recruitment had checked out every single thing about Tom Fairwood, right down to his third grade report card and what he ate for breakfast, and he was in no way related to me. Otherwise he wouldn't be here.

I said, "Gorgeous view, isn't it?"

"I always find looking at this so calming."

We went through the rest of the inane identification protocol, and then I made my decision. "Change of plans, Tom. You're coming with me."

"Has something happened that—"

"I'll tell you on the way. Come on."

He strode along beside me, not asking further questions, just obeying. A good sign. We walked to the car like two people, possibly mother and son, out to enjoy the weather, occasionally exchanging a trivial remark.

In my car Tom said, "Are we going to a station?"

"No. You're going to meet our cell leader."

He nodded and said nothing more until we pulled up to Kyle Washington's house in the Seattle suburb of Burien.

It was not my job to train Tom. The recruiter, whom I of course didn't know, would have done that. Tom would already know everything important: why we were organized the way we were, the security measures we had to take, the reporting rules, the kinds of tasks he would perform. My job was to assign him those tasks. I was the third-in-command in our cell of the Org, a grandiose position for a group of four people—now, five. Only Kyle, our cell leader, knew where other cells were. If Kyle was hit by a bus, his second, "Jonas," would report to one of the scientists at one of the four stations our cell covered and receive further instructions from him or her.

The Org had to be set up that way. When its predecessor group hadn't been, soon after the Catastrophe, the result was that the entire original group had been discovered and prosecuted under RICO statutes. Some members had flipped; dozens had gone to jail; two people had committed suicide; and Dr. Eric Kitson, founder, had died in a hail of FBI bullets when he walked, unarmed but without his hands raised, out of a station. No FBI agents were ever prosecuted for that murder.

For our carefully rebuilt resistance movement,

secrecy and planning were key. A relatively small number of people can effect huge change if they're well organized. In 1917, just 23,000 Communist Party members eventually seized control of a government controlling 180 million peasants. A tiny handful of terrorists brought down the World Trade Center towers.

In the Org (the only name it had), recruitment was rigorous. No communications were digital. Everything was on a need-to-know basis, and hardly anyone knew anyone else. Certainly I didn't. I didn't even know how big the Org was in total, although I suspected it had grown pretty large since Kyle had once let slip a reference to "regional headquarters." Which, of course, implied a nonregional headquarters somewhere. That was a small nugget of knowledge I was not supposed to have.

Kyle, on the other hand, did not know about the much larger nugget I possessed. And I was not going to tell him.

Kyle Tyrone Washington lived under his own name. A six-foot-two African American ex-NFL wide receiver is too noticeable to assume an alias. His wife, Susan, was in the front yard doing whatever you do to flower beds in October. It involved a rake, bags of organic-looking stuff, and a wide straw hat. Susan wasn't one of us, and she didn't know what Kyle did when he wasn't at his legitimate job, which was counseling troubled teens and their even more troubled parents in an office adjoining their small brick home.

"Caro," she said, stripping off gardening gloves. "How nice to see you."

"You, too. Susan, this is Tom. Kyle probably told you about him."

"Oh, yes, another chess protege. But I didn't realize you had a match this afternoon."

"Kyle doesn't. Tom and I do. Susan Washington, Tom Fairwood. I picked up Tom and since we pass you on our way into the city, I thought I'd introduce him to Kyle, if Kyle's between clients. If not, it can wait."

"I'll see." Susan smiled pleasantly at Tom and started for the office. Susan was kind, incurious, and a little dim. I was always surprised that a man like Kyle chose a woman like her, but there's no predicting what strangely assorted couples will marry. Just look at Jake and me.

Kyle and Susan emerged from his office. Susan said, "Can you stay for coffee?"

"Thank you, but we have a scheduled match. Kyle, Tom wants to ask you about Fischer's use of the X-ray attack in the 1963 championship match against Bisguier."

Susan laughed. "I'll leave you chess people to it."

When she was out of earshot, Kyle asked, "What's happened?"

I told him, leaving out the toothbrush in my pocket. "Kyle, do you know anything about that lost house that I should also know?"

"No. I'll find out what I can before the meeting tomorrow morning. Meanwhile, since he's here, you might as well take Tom to the station with you. Introduce him there."

"All right." I didn't ask if, or why, Tom could take an overnight trip on such short notice; if he had domestic complications, Kyle wouldn't have told me to take him. "And I need another D. I had to swallow mine at the wandering house."

"You go through a lot of these, Caro. They don't grow on trees, you know. Not yet."

"Ha ha," I said.

Kyle gave his usual wintry smile. His face wore a permanently pained expression, even though he wasn't a pessimistic person. A passionate idealist, he thought the Org could succeed in its mission. I tried to share his belief, because I so desperately wanted to. Sometimes, I even succeeded.

Kyle brought me another D from a safe some-where deep in the house. Back in my car, Tom said, "Do you know a lot about chess?"

"Nothing at all," I said. "I've memorized some

sentences to drive Susan away. You'll need to do the same. I'll give you a—"

"You don't have to," he said. "I held a 2100 ranking in college."

I nodded and concentrated on driving to I-90, eyes on the road, expression blank. Ian, too, had played chess. After ten years, memory was no longer a tsunami swamping everything else in my mind, but the slow, dark tides it brought were sometimes worse. And thinking of Ian meant, inevitably, thinking of Jake, who would never see this kid beside me who looked so much like our lost son. Although, considering everything that had happened both between us and around us, maybe that was a good thing.

But still, Jake's loss. And mine. One of so many, starting from practically the day we met.

2005: NEW HAVEN, CONNECTICUT

"I'M NOT GOING," I said to Dena.

My roommate turned in our dorm room at Yale and glared at me. "Why not?"

"Because it's trivial."

"Theater isn't trivial! Come on, Renata, lighten up. Oh, wait—you don't know how to lighten up."

I turned away, marveling for the hundredth time at the stupidity of campus housing, which had put me in a room with Dena only because her preferred roommate had abruptly left school to get married (also stupid—who gets married at twenty-one?), and I had been too busy with things that actually mattered to turn in my housing forms. Dena, from somewhere in Kentucky, was smart, funny, and completely without boundaries. She took my clothes, cursed in class, smoked (nobody at Yale smoked), and resisted assimilation into the Ivy League with every inch of her perpetually overexposed body. She also maintained an A-minus GPA. And when she wanted something, she had the tenacity of a wood tick.

"Dena, I'm not going to the play with you. I like theater, yes, but only good theater. Not stupid farce, which this play is."

"It's Molière. You'd go with me if the drama department were doing it in French. Then it would be sophisticated enough for you, even if you only understood every fifth word."

She could display an annoying penetration that never failed to disconcert me, especially since it usually held a barb.

I said, "But it's not in French, is it? And I have to study." I had arrived two weeks late on campus, with the dean's permission, and was way behind.

Dena changed tactics. She laid her hand on my arm. "Renata, please please please. You're my only friend on campus—" not true, but close "—and I don't want to go alone."

"It's that guy, isn't it? That blond actor you're trying to hook up with. You're still chasing him."

"I'm not chasing him. I'm trying to get him to chase me, and it's too obvious if I go backstage alone. Anyway, he has a nice friend, and you and the friend are both from Portland. There's a bond right there."

"I'm from Seattle."

"Same thing."

"I's not even the same *state*."

"Whatever. Also, you're both here on scholarship."

"Dena—"

"Okay, forget the friend. I never even met him anyway. Look, if you just do this one teeny tiny thing for me, I'll write that paper you owe in Contemporary Brit Lit."

The paper was due in three days, I was drowning in work, and I couldn't remember why I had chosen Contemporary Brit Lit as my last senior-year elective. Dena was an English major.

"Okay," I said, "I'll go. But just to watch the play and make one quick trip backstage. I'm not going drinking with you guys, if you even get that far."

"I will. And thank you, thank you, thank you!"

"Don't gush and simper, Dena, it doesn't work on me. And give me back that shirt!"

"I wasn't going to wear it anyway," she said scornfully. "Not to *this*." She took off my button-down and put on a clingy, low-cut tee with her jeans.

My jeans. But I let it go. I needed that Brit Lit paper.

After *Tartuffe*, which was just as silly as I remembered, we made our way backstage. The blond actor playing Orgon was immediately accosted by Dena. I was plotting escape when Tartuffe came up to me, still in costume and makeup.

"Hi, I'm Jake Sanderson. Renata, right? I think we're going out with Alan and Dena."

"I don't think so," I said, inwardly furious at Dena's duplicity. Then, to make up for my rudeness, I added, "You were good in the play." It was true: his Tartuffe had an oily slyness that never slipped into overexaggeration. He'd dominated even those scenes where he stood in the background. Not classically handsome, he had presence, plus the priceless asset of a truly compelling voice, like that old-time actor Richard Burton. But American instead of British.

"I was more than good," he said, "I was spectacular. And eventually I'm going to be even better."

"All that and modesty, too," I said, turned off but also surprised. Yale, God knew, had its share of outsized egos, but usually there were token attempts to keep them hidden.

"Fact trumps modesty," he said. "Look, Renata, come out with us. Dena told me what you've been doing for the last month. I'm intrigued."

Bile rose in my throat. "Intrigued? You're intrigued by the 2,000 deaths and thousands of homeless and sheer misery caused by Hurricane

Katrina? You're not appalled by the way the government mishandled the crisis? You're not outraged or, at a minimum, compassionate for the victims?"

"All of that. None of which means I can't also be intrigued that a Yale senior would arrive so late on campus because she was in Louisiana with Second Harvest, feeding displaced persons. I thought Dena told me you had a logical mind."

"And I thought you were good as Tartuffe but no Hal Holbrook."

"So you saw the old TV movie! Your artistic purity isn't quite as pure as you pretend. And actually, you did think I was as good as Holbrook. Do you think I can't tell? And just because you're a junior activist and I'm a not-yet-famous actor doesn't mean you can't have a drink with me."

"But why would you want to?" I wasn't flirting; I never flirted. I genuinely wanted to know. Most guys were put off by me. *You come on too strong*, Dena once told me. *There's a fine line between confidence and abrasiveness.* I'd replied that I don't toe lines.

Jake said, "Damned if I know why I want to have a drink with you. Let's find out."

———————

Let's find out. That became the mantra for our lives. The chief things we found out were about each other. All senior year we dated, fucked, and fought. It got to the point that I couldn't tell the three things apart. We fought on dates; we fucked while fighting; we dated at events that were the subjects of our fights. I coordinated demonstrations for disability rights and against the Middle East wars. And Jake, who was supposed to attend a big demonstration with me, missed it because the drama department held an emergency rehearsal of a Shaw play after Saint Joan came down with flu two days before opening night. I missed the opening night of *Bus Stop*, in which Jake played Bo, because I was marching in Florida for immigrant rights. We had angry sex, we had make-up sex, we had tender sex, we had sex so full of laughter that we nearly rolled off the bed in Jake's ratty apartment.

In May we graduated, me with a degree in Poli Sci and Jake in theater. Both of our families came east for graduation. The one dinner we all had together was not a success. Jake's mother, a widow, wore a fussy polyester dress and asked the Lord to help us to victory in Iraq. My parents, old and unrepentant hippies, wore jeans and handmade wooden jewelry and talked about the fight to legalize marijuana. Dylan, Jake's teenage brother, made rude remarks and sneered at everything.

After dinner, to erase the strain, Jake and I went back to his room and had more sex.

Two days later, Jake left for New York to try his luck as an actor. I went to D.C. to work for the Environmental Protection Agency as a one-year intern, where I did nothing of significance. We commuted, argued, broke up, got back together.

In 2007, Jake got the role of Valentine in a regional production of *Arcadia* and went to Dallas. I got fed up with photocopying and answering phones. I quit the EPA, which didn't seem to me to be protecting much of anything, and went to work for Planned Parenthood. I also arranged demonstrations for the Matthew Shepard Act, against the air strikes in Somalia, and for animal rights.

In April, Jake and I broke up. "You don't even know why you're an activist!" he flung at me in the heat of battle. "Your 'causes' are all over the map. You like the fight more than the cause—any cause—because it makes you feel important and alive!"

"You don't understand the first thing about me!" I screamed back. "And you never will!"

In 2008, the economy collapsed. I went to work for the Obama campaign in Chicago. Jake got a small part off-Broadway and was mentioned glowingly in nearly every review of the play. After the presidential election, I moved to

New York, got rehired by Planned Parenthood, and narrowly avoided arrest during a counterprotest at an abortion clinic. We started seeing each other again. The sex was still spectacular.

That year, Jake and I broke up twice, the second time on New Year's Eve. I was planning a January contraception push for high school girls. He was supposed to leave for a screen test in Hollywood. I refused to go with him. "If you have to make movies, at least go to Europe where they make decent art films! Don't waste any more of your life than you already have!"

Afterward, I regretted saying that. Even my twenty-five-year-old self knew that I was a prig. But it was too late. Jake stalked out of the party just as people began singing "Auld Lang Syne," and we were over.

That night, I couldn't sleep at all. I drank vodka, my numbing solution of choice, until a watery sun rose over Manhattan. Missing Jake this time wasn't like missing him other times. Somewhere in the deepest caves of my mind, I'd known that our other break-ups weren't permanent. I'd known it the way you know that your broken elbow will heal, your sprained wrist will eventually lift things again. But then your whole arm is amputated, both wrist and elbow gone for good, and you must learn to live without them.

I did all the things you do when you hope

someone will contact you. I checked my texts every five minutes. I set my computer volume on loud so that anywhere in the apartment, I would hear notification of an email from Jake Sanderson. I followed his Facebook page compulsively, which was how I knew he was getting small movie parts and dating an unimportant Hollywood actress with blond hair to her waist.

But I didn't call him. He was in the wrong; he should have been the one to call me.

The incredible, self-spiting arrogance of the young.

2032: SEATTLE, WASHINGTON

THE ORG STATION headed by Dr. Louis Weinberg was in Eastern Washington, over the Cascade Mountains that split the state into two regions so different from each other that they might as well be separate countries. Seattle was wet, liberal, full of sharp contrasts: tech rich who owned drivies. Two- or four-person quadcopter taxis. Delivery drones for anything that you didn't mind being hacked. Armed home-protection bots. Most of all, food security. The shrinking middle class, who owned the independent services catering to the tech rich, also could afford enough nutritious food. Everybody else, made jobless and sometimes homeless by automation, survived on cheap, starchy food donated by agribusinesses, who were reimbursed by governments state and federal. It was nice for the agribusinesses. It also prevented outright revolution. So far.

Beneath the underpasses of the expressway, the homeless encampments had grown even larger than when I last drove I-90 to Louis' station. Police drones darted in and out.

As we sped past the heavily fortified mansions on the east side of Lake Washington, Tom broke the silence in my car. "What can you tell me about the station we're going to?"

"Nothing until we get there," I said. "Protocol. You talk to me instead. You heard what I told Kyle about the lost house. Nobody was in it. The Org uses drivie houses very selectively, and they're never left empty. So what do you think might have happened, and with what consequences?"

Tom knew I was testing him, that I wanted to assess how bright he was, that I hadn't been impressed by his chess rating. He probably even knew that I didn't understand his chess rating. All that was in his grin, which disappeared as he ordered his thoughts.

"The agent either left the house by choice or was taken by force. If the agent defected or was an infiltrator to the Org, his or her destination might be a group that hates us. If the agent was kidnapped or arrested, then it was also by a group that hates us. Either way, it's not good. Any agent assigned a drivie house is higher up in the Org than you and so can probably identify more than one or two stations."

"Maybe."

We stayed silent all through the climb into the mountains to Snoqualmie Pass, while I ran through the list of groups that hated us.

The environmental groups, of course. Since the Catastrophe, they'd proliferated like kudzu. They came in all sizes from international to very local, all degrees of militant from Greenpeace to let's-write-more-letters-to-our-congressman. Greenpeace was militant, all right. But just before the Catastrophe ten years ago, their leadership had been charged under RICO statutes with the murder of a whaler, and ever since, they'd been far more careful. A kidnapping to torture for information just didn't seem their style. Of course that didn't rule out smaller eco-groups, some of whom were batshit crazy.

The religious right hated us. It was conceivable that they'd twisted an obscure Bible verse into a justification for some sort of "cleansing." But again, if that had happened, it would probably be a breakaway local sect that had gone straight off the rails.

Agribusiness hated us the way they hated anything that interfered with profits, which we would do eventually—but not yet, not in any significant way. Was some rogue, well-informed CEO anticipating that?

The big enemy of course was DAS—the Department of Agricultural Security that the president had created after the Catastrophe. A cabinet-level secretary, close ties with the FBI, all the funding that could be carved out of anywhere else on a strained federal budget. If DAS had arrested our lost-house agent, then the feds could detain him or her indefinitely as a "material witness." DAS would do whatever it needed to in order to obtain information, to "prevent another Catastrophe and protect the American people." The Org would have to take on DAS eventually, but not this soon, and not like this. We weren't ready.

Finally—maybe it wasn't an organization at all. Maybe the lost-house agent had been killed by a burglar who'd taken away the body, or kidnapped by a scorned girlfriend, a scorned boyfriend, a random psycho. Nothing to do with us. Coincidences happened, after all, and even our agents had private lives. Undoubtedly someone farther up our chain of command knew, or would discover from police contacts, if the wandering-house murder was personal. Just as Org command knew all about everything personal about me and Jake, right down to the last division of furniture and dishes during our divorce.

If so, the Org would not tell me. I wasn't important enough. I trusted my higher-ups.

So why had I taken the toothbrush? And then not told Kyle?

Tom asked, "Can you at least tell me what they're doing at the station we're checking on?"

"Carrots," I said. "They're doing carrots."

The central part of Eastern Washington is more than 2,000 feet in elevation, dry high plains. Drier since global warming began to accelerate. Even in October, I had the AC on full blast as Tom and I drove up to the station run by Dr. Louis Weinberg.

"This is it," I said, pointing to the small farmhouse, family vegetable garden, and apple orchard that were decoys, and the two small greenhouses that were not. Jean met us at the end of the driveway, smiling widely when she saw me.

"Hello, Caroline. Good to see you."

"And you. This is my cell's new recruit, Tom Fairwood. Tom, 'Jean Cathcart,' plant geneticist." Only one scientist at each station used their real names, in order to access online scientific journals and to order equipment and restricted supplies, although not to this address. The farmhouse was owned by someone else. I didn't know who; I didn't need to know.

"Hi, Tom. Caro, did you bring that shipment of supplies?"

"In the trunk."

The three of us carried smallish cardboard boxes labeled "Maternity Clothes" into the house. One of them actually did contain maternity clothes, in case I was stopped by the police and had to explain that I was collecting them for charity. We set the boxes down in the small kitchen and Louis came through from the back of the house. Tom blinked at what lay behind the open doorway.

When the door was closed, it was completely hidden by shallow shelves holding cookbooks, dishes, pottery, a carved wooden rooster. The kitchen appeared like what any unwanted visitor would expect: copper-bottomed pans hung on the wall, a window over the sink looking out into the orchard, a house-system Link sitting on a shelf, ready to take commands about remembering dental appointments or ordering more milk. Blue cotton curtains at the windows, dirty dishes in the sink, calendar with "Great Moments in American History" on the wall. No one had turned the page from September to October.

Beyond the kitchen was the small, windowless, state-of-the-art lab. The heavy-duty genetic work was done elsewhere and brought here by couriers like me, but Louis and Jean and their assistant, Miguel, also did a fair amount of work here. Each piece of expensive equipment had been brought in separately, by night, over time. The clutter and homey neglect of the kitchen contrasted starkly with the lab. Tom scrutinized everything.

I was wary around new recruits, even though I knew the Org was insanely careful and it wasn't my place to second-guess their decisions Still, I always wondered—will this be the one who betrays us?

Louis came forward, holding out his hand. "Louis Weinberg. I run this root-vegetable circus."

"Tom Fairwood. I know you and Caroline have things to talk about—but can I get a tour?"

"Of course. Briefly, anyway." Louis, too, was watching Tom carefully, weighing him. How bright was he, how curious, how potentially useful? Louis didn't miss much. Soft-spoken, genial, bald as an egg, glasses in heavy dark frames—he looked like an inoffensive professor of eighteenth-century literature. He was a scientist of blazing brilliance, fire under cool snow. Beneath that genial and laid-back manner was the sharpest mind I knew. Also dark currents I sensed but didn't understand. I knew his professional background, including his "retirement" from researching for a major agribusiness, but my contacts with Louis were too limited for me to understand him, even though I have good instincts about people.

(*Jake shouting, "No, you don't! You only think you do!"*

Fuck you, Jake.)

"This is the lab, and we can see the greenhouse after. How much do you know about genemod crop creation, Tom?"

"I've been reading what I can."

I demanded, "Where?"

"Not online," he said. "In libraries. Not checking out books."

I nodded. Everything online, including book purchases and library checkouts, could be datamined to show patterns of interest in genetic engineering. That might alert DAS. Nothing anywhere on any layer of the internet is safe for us. Nor are phone calls, patterns of purchase, patterns of approval on social media, or pretty much anything else digital. Louis read scientific journals at various libraries scattered over four counties.

Louis said, as if I hadn't thrust my rude suspicions into the middle of his lecture, "This station is working on carrots. As you probably know, genuine biohacking proved a lot harder than was expected twenty-five or thirty years ago. All those amateurs experimenting with supply-store genes almost never ended up with organisms that were self-perpetuating, useful, and what they planned. The Catastrophe, you'll remember, wasn't caused by basement amateurs."

Of course Tom remembered; everybody remembered. I trailed after Louis, hoping he wasn't going to turn too pedantic. He pointed out to Tom major pieces of lab equipment and the strictly offline computers; one of my jobs was to hand-carry data on very small drive cubes that could, like Ds, be swallowed, if necessary. So far, I had not had to test this.

"What you really want to see is in the greenhouses," Louis said. "This way."

Outside, sun poured down from a bright blue sky. Instinctively, I scanned for drones. Nothing. Space-satellite surveillance would show three people walking to an ordinary greenhouse on a lovely October day.

"Carrots are great sources of beta carotene, which contains vitamin A," Louis said. "Every year nearly a million children worldwide go blind from vitamin A deficiency, and within a year of blindness, half of those die. Vitamin A deficiency also affects the immune system, making it harder to fight infections. Before the Catastrophe, an organization called the Global Alliance for Vitamin A distributed the vitamin steadily in the poorest parts of the world, but then that ceased. You can't imagine the devastation and suffering among those children."

"Yes," Tom said. "I can. I've seen it."

Louis stopped dead at the greenhouse door and stared at him. "You have? Where? Africa? India? No, never mind—you probably can't say. Sorry." He opened the door of the first greenhouse.

Tom was, I'd been told, twenty-three. Where and how had he been in Asia or Africa? It wasn't like travel between countries was easy anymore, not since the Catastrophe. Military duty, maybe. What else didn't I know about Tom Fairwood?

The greenhouse transported us away from Eastern Washington. Instead of semi-arid high plains, we were in a hot, humid coastal region; I could actually smell salt in the air, as if a breeze blew off an ocean. Raised beds of carrots, along with a few of Queen Anne's lace, crowded the space. I once speculated with another Org member about the rumor that in a DAS raid, stations and growth beds were wired to explode, destroying all evidence. Neither of us had had any idea whether that was true. I still didn't, but I doubted it. We hid from the feds, but we weren't an espionage or paramilitary group, just a bunch of civilians trying to covertly save the world.

One carrot at a time.

"These are Danvers carrots," Louis said. He caressed a leafy green stalk as if he were its lover, which I found a little creepy. But that was Louis. He continued, "Danvers can handle heavy soil better than most, although ideally all carrots need loose, deep soil or they grow stunted. Carrots have only moderate tolerance for salt, and we're modifying these to grow in water with as much as 3,000 parts per million. Coastal land in the developing world and even in California is increasingly being invaded by the rising sea. If we succeed, those places will be able to grow our carrots and then store them in tubs of sand for winter use. We're also modifying them for increased beta carotene and to resist both vegetable soft rot and leaf blight. *Without* the use of pesticides or fungicides. Leaf blight is the most widespread carrot disease, poor things." Again he caressed the delicate stalk.

Tom watched this performance without reacting, for which I gave him credit. He said, "Why the bed of Queen Anne's lace?"

"They're closely related to carrots, both *Daucus carota*." He didn't need to say more to bring the Catastrophe to everyone's mind. "Come to the other greenhouse. You'll be amazed."

Amazement in the second greenhouse consisted of a hotter, drier climate than even outdoors, and more carrots. The sweat that had started on my neck, forehead, and bra line in the ersatz coastal region didn't evaporate. Miguel, doing something on a back bench, waved to me. Louis made the introductions and added, "Carrots like full sunlight and hot weather, but of course they need water. We're modifying these to require the barest minimum so they can be planted in semi-arid regions or those experiencing bad drought. If they'd had these in Ethiopia in 2024 . . ." He shook his head sadly. "Norman Borlaug once said, 'Most of the people who are opposing biotechnology have never known hunger.' I'd add, 'or vitamin deficiency diseases.'"

"Louis," Miguel said, "a quick question."

The question wasn't quick, and so technical that I didn't even try to follow it. As they discussed, Tom turned to me. "They're not using the Blanding vectors in their genemods?"

"No. Newer techniques. Don't ask Louis what, because you don't need to know."

"Got it."

Glad to escape the greenhouses, I collected the written material to convey to Kyle, who would relay it up the Org's chain of command. Once, people called "mules" carried illegal drugs in their intestines across national borders. I'm an updated version of a mule, but at least I don't have to swallow anything except a D, unless I'm caught. If I am, Louis' report is written on thin, easy-to-chew paper, folded small. Spectacularly low-tech, and secure as digital never was. I put the report in my pocket, told Tom to wait in the car, and sought out Jean. She was in the kitchen, making dinner. It smelled good.

"Want to stay?" Jean asked. "There's plenty."

"Thanks, but we need to get back. A word, please?"

I led the way outside, to the apple orchard. The

abrupt dark of a Northwest October was descending. Small, annoying bugs whirred around our heads. A half moon hung over the plains, and the air had grown chilly. I wrapped my arms around myself.

"Jean, I need something, and I don't want Louis to know."

"Why not?" I couldn't see her face, but I felt her looking at me hard.

"I can't tell you that." And then I did something I've never done before: I lied to an Org member. "It's Kyle's request."

"Okay." That one word said she didn't like this but would do it if it came from Kyle.

From my pocket I pulled the toothbrush I'd taken in the wandering house. "Can you generate a DNA sequence on the saliva from this? I'll pick it up next week."

"And then Kyle will have someone with medical or police access run it through databases for a match?"

"Yes, I think so. He didn't tell me that."

"No, he wouldn't. But why can't Louis know? Louis isn't under suspicion of anything, is he? Not Louis!"

"No, of course not." Whatever had happened to the Org agent in the lost house, it was inconceivable that Louis Weinberg could have anything to do with it. "But you know how Louis is. Laser focus when his attention is caught. Maybe Kyle doesn't want him distracted from carrots."

"Maybe," Jean said, but her tone said she wasn't convinced by my feeble justification. But the order supposedly came from Kyle, so she took the toothbrush, now wrapped in a tissue, and put it in her pocket.

To turn her attention, I said, "I'd be interested in your impressions of Tom."

To my surprise, she said, "I don't really trust him."

"You don't? Why not? He must have been thoroughly vetted by recruitment."

"They can miss things, you know. Anaheim."

Two years ago an entire cell of the Org had been infiltrated, betrayed, and arrested in Anaheim. They were still in jail, and we'd lost all their research on genetically modified fig trees.

Jean continued, "I don't have anything definite to say about Tom. It's just a feeling. But I have good instincts about people."

That was *my* line. Besides, if Jean really had such good instincts, she'd know I was lying about Kyle's orders.

We said our good byes and Tom and I drove back to Seattle. Drivies passed us; I never risked attracting drone attention by exceeding the speed limit. Tom asked, "Will I be running courier for this station now?"

"If Kyle says so."

"When do we visit the next station? No, never mind, I know—when Kyle says so."

"That's right." I was courier for three of the cell's four stations, but that didn't mean Tom would be, or at least not right away. Jonas was my backup and I was his, but since cells usually consisted of four people and now we had five, that argued that Jonas was being groomed for leadership elsewhere. Which would make sense, because all of us, including Jonas, had expected that he would be made leader of this cell. Instead, Kyle, whom none of us knew, had been brought in from the outside.

Maybe now Jonas would get his promotion. Obscurely, I was glad it was him and not me.

No, not obscurely. I didn't want a transfer to another part of the country. Not while I had a fourth . . . no, not a station, although I sometimes thought of it that way. The one that not even Kyle knew about. The one that had saved my life.

Tom interrupted my musing, loudly. "Caroline? Did you hear me? I asked if you're hungry."

And all at once, I was. The last thing I'd put in my stomach had been beer in the café balcony at Pioneer Square. "Sure. Want to stop? There's a diner about twenty miles ahead, just off the expressway."

The diner was nearly empty. Before drivie

trucks, the place probably had had more custom-ers. Before the Catastrophe, it probably also had had a better menu. I was surprised that the own-ers, who might have been the sullen cook and lone, aged waitress, had hung on at all. An eco-nomic crash had winners and losers, and these looked like losers.

Sitting across from me in the booth, Tom frowned at the menu, which was paper instead of electronic inlay. "Pretty limited."

"Well—"

"I was hoping for seafood, which I guess was dumb considering where we are. I love clams. Do you?"

He'd raised his head to smile at me, and alarm bells clanged in my head. What did he know? Was his question a signal . . . but of what? From whom? Or did he want me to know that he'd dis-covered my identity? *Clams* . . .

"No," I said, "I don't like them."

"Oh." He went back to the menu, and I did the same, wondering what expression had been on my face, whether I had given anything away.

And wishing, stupidly, because there was nothing to be done about it, that he didn't remind me so much of Ian. I was not this kid's mother. I would never be anyone's mother again.

2010: PORTLAND, OREGON

CHILDHOOD DOESN'T REALLY END until both your parents die. Before that, even if you are fifty or sixty or seventy, you are still someone's daughter. The older generation, no matter whether you visit them or not, like them or not, take care of them or not, is nonetheless a wall between you and the abyss.

I liked my parents and they'd never needed caretaking. They were only in their fifties, healthy and active, with a lot of friends. At least once a month we had dinner together, me driving down to Portland from Seattle. I'd moved there after the break-up with Jake, unable to bear the memories in Manhattan.

Seattle is a city defined by both the tech industry and crunchy-granola activism. I found a job with a law firm that did a lot of pro bono work, especially on sexual assault cases. I demonstrated for sea lion habitats and against hate speech. I made few friends, by choice. I stayed celibate. The city, gray in January rain, suited me. My parents worried about me, as I never worried about them.

I hoped they hadn't had time to see the twelve-wheeler that lost control on the expressway and hit their Toyota.

The memorial service I'd organized at a funeral home in Portland was thronged. People stood in the back, against the walls, in the hallways. Seven people spoke movingly about "Bea and Jim." Both my parents, like me, had been only children, and the only family present was my ancient Great-Aunt Cecilia, who hung on my neck and wept. I peeled her off, stony-faced. Stone was the only way I could get through this.

"Where is the gathering afterward?" Great-Aunt Cecilia asked.

"There isn't one. I don't live in this city."

She looked shocked. "But, Renata, there's always a gathering afterward! You should have—"

"I didn't," I said shortly, and turned away. My parents had never liked Cecilia, and I didn't see why I should. Nor did I believe in her grief. I didn't know, then, that you don't have to be close to a dead family member to feel mortality hissing at your back.

Afterward, I had to stand in the doorway,

shake hands, and thank everyone. It was torture. My hand grew cramped, my fake smile felt like a death rictus, I tried to evade the hugs I emphatically did not want. When everyone was gone, I closed my eyes to shut out all of it, including the overly helpful funeral director who'd wanted me to sign up for grief counseling.

When I opened my eyes, a cop stood facing me in the doorway.

I stiffened. I'd been arrested twice in the past for protests that got out of hand, and cops are not my favorite people. But . . . this cop looked familiar. Still, I couldn't place him until he spoke. I was always better at voices than faces.

"Renata," he said awkwardly, "I'm sorry about your folks."

"Dylan? Sanderson?"

"Yeah, it's me."

Jake's little brother, whom I'd last seen almost four years ago at my Yale graduation, had grown up. He looked a little like Jake, Jake without the confident swagger or intense eyes, Jake in dim photocopy. Dylan shifted uneasily from one foot to another, a childish gesture at odds with his uniform. Which, I saw now, looked very new.

"Dylan, what are you doing here?"

"The police report came in about your parents' accident. I recognized your name, of course, as next of kin."

Why "of course"? We'd only met that once. I didn't ask him.

"I wasn't very nice to you at Yale," he said. "It was . . . I was . . . anyway, I apologize."

I didn't think a spate of teenage rudeness four years ago required showing up at a funeral in order to apologize, but maybe he thought it did. Tired as I was of considering everybody else today, I still managed another horrible smile. "Don't worry about it."

He didn't look any more comfortable. "Well, I'm glad to hear you say that, because I did something else."

Fuck—now what? Before I could say anything more, Jake strode in from the hallway.

People say, "My stomach jumped," and I always thought it was a metaphor. People say, "I almost fainted," and I dismissed it as hyperbole. Both things can be facts. As I struggled to recover, to turn cold toward both brothers' presumptuousness, Jake had his arms around me in a hug.

"Renata, I'm so so sorry . . . I know you loved them . . . it's so fucking unfair!"

For the first time since the accident, I leaned into someone.

The only thing I remember between that moment and a double Scotch in a dim bar was Dylan's triumphant, smug smile. "*I* did it," he said, and then he was gone, and Jake and I faced each other across a booth, some terrible country-western music droning in the background and the NFL playoffs on the TV over the bar. Green Bay Packers versus Philadelphia Eagles. The Packers were winning.

"Why did you come?" I demanded.

"Same old Renata." Jake reached over to squeeze my fingers. "I came because we were both idiots and I missed you so much I thought my heart would split down its seam."

"What play is that from? And if I remember correctly, you missed me so much you were dating Marilu What's-Her-Name."

"How do you know that?"

"I read it in some supermarket tabloid."

"You never read a tabloid in your life, and neither Marilu nor I am important enough to be in one. You followed me on Facebook. No, don't glare at me, Renata—I followed your Facebook page, too. Every single day—not that you ever said much."

"You did? Then why the fuck didn't you call me?"

"Why didn't *you* call *me*?"

We were glaring at each other now, bristly as

fighting cats. Nobody said anything. The Packers scored a touchdown.

"Okay," I said finally, "it's over now."

"What's over? Our separation or this fight?"

"Which do you want to be over?" In that moment, I think I hated him.

He shook his head, suddenly amused. "You can't back down, can you? Even when you want to." His voice softened. "Even when we both want to. We're together again, Renata. This time, for good."

"Don't you think you should ask me first?"

"You ask me instead."

"No," I said, nodding my head so that it was both no and yes at the same time. And then, before I knew I was going to say anything, "I miss them so much, Jake."

He made an understanding noise, but I knew he didn't really understand. Jake didn't much like his puritanical, self-righteous mother. He hadn't much liked Dylan, either, although perhaps that had changed. There was an in-the-moment quality to Jake that had, I realized, been the source of so many of our fights. Jake gave himself completely to the present, with an underlying disdain for those who wasted the moment. I gave myself to the future, considered his attitude puerile, and resented his disdain. But he sat across from me in that moment, with his whole loving heart in his beautiful, rich actor's voice, and for the first time in a year, my body felt alive again.

"Together," I said. "For good."

It wasn't that easy, of course. I didn't want to leave my job in Seattle. Jake was still getting small parts in Hollywood. We commuted, using up the money my parents had left me. We didn't have too many fights; time together was too precious. We did have a lot of sex, which was just as good as ever. I met a few of his friends, including Marilu, who turned out to be friendly but so ambitious that, even through my jealousy, I could see that no man mattered much to her unless he could help her career. I still didn't have, or want, friends in Seattle, although sometimes Dylan called and said he was driving up anyway and asked whether we could have coffee. I always said yes. Dylan was, from what I could tell, plodding through his job as a rookie cop in Portland, but he said little about it. Unlike Jake, he was a fidgety person, tapping his foot and jiggling his knee and tugging at his ear as we chatted aimlessly about movies or politics. I didn't really enjoy those coffee dates, but he was Jake's brother, and he seemed lonely.

We had been flying back and forth between

Seattle and L.A. for four months when everything happened.

Jake got the second lead in a major picture from Paramount, *Year of the Goat*. It was an incredible part: the alcoholic best friend who knows how pathetic he is, comes through at the end, and sacrifices his own happiness for the woman he loves from afar, the sister of the hero (who is not all that heroic). The role had a wide emotional range that could attract a lot of attention. "I can't believe they gave it to me," Jake kept saying as we celebrated. "I can't fucking *believe* it."

"You'll be great," I said over and over. He would be. The part was made for him.

"But do you know who I beat out for the role? Do you know who else wanted it—how *big* they are?"

"You told me. They chose you. God, Jake, this will be your big break! Kiss me."

He did. Then again, and again, and we were having drunken sex, and I didn't put in my diaphragm. A month later, I Skyped Jake in Hollywood to tell him I was pregnant. He turned pale.

"Renata . . . how do . . . it isn't . . . what do you want to do?"

"I don't know." I was confused, sick every morning, assisting with a tricky case at work, peeing urgently at inconvenient times. My body had always been strong and reliable; sickness was alien to me.

"I'll do whatever you want," Jake said, and I knew that he was afraid of losing his big chance. That made me angry.

"Do you think I'd ever interfere with your movie? Knowing how much you want it? That's really insulting, Jake!"

"Don't get mad. It's just . . ."

"Just what?" I wanted to throw something at him. I wanted to go again to the bathroom. I wanted to cry. I never cry.

He said, "Just that I want to marry you and have this baby, and I'm afraid you'll say no."

Did he mean it? I'll never really know. Pregnancy hurried along the marriage that might have happened naturally—or not. Hurry sometimes isn't a good thing. But I did know he loved me, and two days later we flew to Las Vegas and got married. I threw up immediately before and immediately after the ceremony.

"How will marriage be?" I asked, wiping my mouth outside the ladies' room at the Office of Civil Marriages.

Jake, ashen, managed a grin. "Let's find out."

The next day, I flew back to Seattle, and Jake went to Hollywood.

I had a difficult pregnancy. Morning sickness persisted all day. "It will stop after the first trimester," my doctor said. It didn't. Unable to keep food down, I developed an iron deficiency. Jake came from Hollywood when he could, which wasn't often. I refused to go down there and puke on the set or in a hotel room, away from my doctor. Part of *Year of the Goat* was shot on location in North Carolina, and all we could do was Skype. I was bewildered—this person with a little parasite growing in her, this vomity, weak person, was not me. I didn't know myself. Other women had easy, even glowing pregnancies. I felt cheated.

The weather in North Carolina did not cooperate. The movie went over schedule, over budget. After Jake's movie wrapped, he was in Seattle more, but not a lot more. The shoot had generated a lot of buzz, but MGM was keeping postproduction under tight control. Jake had to be in Hollywood to record looping, to go to auditions and screen tests, to have conferences with producers and his agent, Morgan Tarryn. Jake wasn't yet major tabloid fodder, so nobody investigated his personal life.

Did I resent that he was with me so little? Yes. Did I know he couldn't help it? Yes. Did I resent having to take a leave of absence from my job while Jake was glorying in his? Yes. That, too, wasn't his fault. But it drove us a little apart.

I developed preeclampsia and had to stay in

bed. Outside my small, dark apartment, rain fell incessantly. Terrified of losing the baby, I got out of bed only to go to the bathroom, shower once a day, and stack the day's food by my bedside. I took about half of Jake's calls and let the rest go to voicemail.

Ian was born six weeks premature, in late-November rain gloomy even for Seattle. I went alone to the hospital, in a taxi. I don't think the driver even knew I was pregnant; I'd vomited so much during the pregnancy that the baby bump under my coat wasn't obvious, and the pains weren't yet bad.

I expected a hard labor to match my hard pregnancy, but Ian slid easily into the world. He was small but healthy; he was perfect. I held him next to me and felt the world shake beneath my bed, beneath the hospital, beneath the universe. Everything shifted. From that moment, Ian became the most important thing in the entirety of creation.

Jake arrived the next day with apologies and roses and exclamations of love, and I showed off the baby, and laughed with Jake, and knew that he had gone into second place in my heart.

November 2010. The Catastrophe that would change the United States was already beginning, on a farm in Indiana. But we didn't know that then. It would be a dozen more years before we, or anyone, knew that. By then, it would be way too late.

2032: SEATTLE, WASHINGTON

WHEN TOM AND I showed up at the cell meeting, the others were already there.

Before we drove to the meeting, I switched identities at a Keep It Safe! The chain of facilities rented lockboxes to people who didn't want to show the identification required for bank safe-deposit boxes. That's lot of people in the age when anything digital can be hacked. Keep It Safe! buildings were ubiquitous, large, and secure, as long as you paid your fee every six months. They asked no questions, accepted cash, and had armed security bots.

Every time I stopped being Renata Black and became Caroline Denton, minion of the Org, I left my government-issued ID and usual cell phone in a lockbox. I traded them an Org-forged ID, a cheap cell phone without net access, and a tiny box with Context Eyes. These—expensive, illegal, handmade—fitted into my eyes and gave me a different retinal scan than Renata's. Law enforcement, of course, knew about Contexts, which was why retinal scans were going out of style. Still, as long as there was a chance I might be casually scanned, I wore them. If I were actually arrested, the Contexts would be discovered, and I'd be made to remove them. I did not plan on being actually arrested.

Tom said, "I switched already," and I nodded. Where, and from what actual identity, was not my business.

The meeting place for our cell was a "suite" in a dilapidated old building in Seattle's industrial district. The building consisted of five floors of studios for artists who never sold a painting, offices of barely-hanging-on businesses, storage areas, and empty rooms. Our suite consisted of a tiny outer room and a larger room behind it. The bathroom was down the hall. We were on the fifth floor. A sign on the door said PARKSIDE CHESS CLUB: MEMBERS ONLY. There was no park, of course, no sign at street level, and no elevator, all of which meant we didn't get drop-ins eager to play chess.

Nonetheless, we had plausible deniability: three small tables with cheap chess sets, three chess clocks, and a large wall poster with photos or drawings of every world champion since

1886 (Wilhelm Steinitz, a singularly ugly man). A splintery wooden counter held a rule book and three other paperbacks detailing famous games. These sat next to the coffee machine and the top one was stained with someone's spilled coffee, making the title impossible to read.

"You're late," said Kyle, who was never late for anything.

"Traffic accident on I-90."

"Drivies or real cars?" asked Jonas, who still distrusted drivies.

"A real car," I said. "Meet Tom Fairwood, our new recruit. Tom, this is Jonas Li and April Shaunessy."

"April May Shaunessy," she said.

April was goofy. In some ways, she reminded me of my long-ago college roommate, Dena. April May chose her Org alias herself, and I didn't know why she was allowed to do that, except that the computer people had special privileges because the rest of us didn't understand what they did. She ran our cell's section of the internet information-and-disinformation campaign. She did it on a computer system in some undisclosed location, using remote servers, remailers somewhere in Eastern Europe, a virtual private network, and tactics that let her posts be read without leading authorities to her. Some of her posts were designed to be hacked, which they were. She planted favorable information about genetic engineering and unfavorable information about those groups opposed to it, including DAS. Some of the disinformation was true, some not. One of her untrue tactics was to say that agribusinesses had been used by foreign powers to destroy the American economy during the Catastrophe. April was good at conspiracy theories, or at least it sounded that way to me. I found the Org's online activities distasteful, even though I knew that our enemies did the same thing. In my apartment I never used the internet except to access the most reliable news channels. Such as they were.

April was Tom's age, pretty in a gamine sort of way, and always slightly off—there was something weird about the way she perceived the world. I didn't know why she'd joined the Org, and so I didn't actually trust her, but Kyle did, and so here she was.

Jonas was different. Quiet, heavyset, balding, he was a biology professor at the University of Washington—I wasn't supposed to know that—with a wife and grown kids. He was risking a lot for the Org because he believed in its goals completely. I didn't understand why he'd been passed over for cell leader in favor of Kyle, but it wasn't my place to question that.

"Now that we're all here," Kyle said, looking at me pointedly, "let's have the monthly reports."

It is possible to care passionately about a cause and yet be bored by other people's participation in it. Nobody was interested in the monthly reports beyond knowing that the work was proceeding. April detailed her disinformation campaign, including far too many technical details. Jonas and I reported on the stations we linked to, without information that would let the others know where the stations were located. All of us were waiting for Kyle to talk about the wandering house.

"Okay," he finally said. "Here's what I can tell you—" which was certainly not all he knew "—about the empty house that Caro entered in Pioneer Square. It *was* one of ours, and there was supposed to be an agent in it. I can't tell you his name, but—"

"Do you know his name?" April blurted out.

"I can't tell you that, either. Come on, April, you know better. I'm sharing everything I can. Nobody in the Org, not all the way to the top, knows what happened to the agent. We have to believe he was arrested, was kidnapped, or defected. We have people checking to see which."

How would we know which? That knowledge implied that somewhere up the chain of command, there were lawyers who didn't operate in the shadows, and maybe also sympathizers in law enforcement. In the FBI? They handled kidnappings, after all.

We all knew better than to ask. But it was a tantalizing glimpse into how far the Org extended.

Kyle said, "What you need to know now is that the Org couldn't find any connection between this cell and the wandering house. It wasn't local. We wouldn't have been told about it at all if Caroline hadn't happened to be there."

Everyone looked at me. I said irritably, "Don't blame me for a coincidence."

Kyle said, "Nobody's blaming you for anything. And you didn't endanger us. It was one just of those things."

"Irrational," April said. "People *are* irrational. Once I was at this lecture by a physicist who was talking about the bread-loaf theory of time. That's when you think about time as a loaf of bread, and if you slice it on the diagonal instead of straight across, then events that we think are in 'the past'—" her fingers made air quotes "—are actually still happening concurrent with the present. The equations support that. Anyway, this woman in the audience got really upset because the woman's daughter had died in a horrific mudslide in California and the woman thought— irrationally!—that the bread-loaf theory meant her daughter was still dying in the present that horrific death that—"

"All right, April, we're moving on now," Kyle

said. He didn't look at me. Kyle was the only one here who knew about Ian.

Beneath the table, I clenched one hand into a fist and reminded myself that April had an IQ of 160 and was essential to our goals.

Kyle said, "Now, the next order of business. . . ."

Throughout the rest of the meeting, I watched Tom, knowing what he was thinking: *This* was the dangerous organization that was going to restore genetic engineering to a country that had rejected it, and so feed both the United States and the world as climate change, desertification, and rising seas changed the face of the globe? This low-key, droning meeting? Where was the adventure and risk taking? Where was the glamour of heroic rebellion?

". . . the expense report with regard to the fund allotment for September . . ."

Tom would learn. We had all learned. The danger, and the accomplishment, was in the details.

While Tom looked disappointed, and April thought of something weird (eyes closed and lips moving silently), and Jonas listened soberly, I felt guilt. I had taken the toothbrush from the wandering house and asked Jean to run a DNA sequence on it, solely because I wanted more knowledge than the Org was willing to give me. I wanted to know who the missing agent was and why he was missing. It wasn't that I didn't trust the Org but that I didn't trust any situation where I didn't know as much as I possibly could.

Not since Ian.

As soon as I walked into the office the next day, my boss said, "Renata, don't take off your jacket. A new case just came in, at the Quinault Nation. They asked for you."

"Tell me."

When Jeremy didn't answer right away, I repeated, "*Tell* me. And are you going with me?"

"Can't. I'm in court this morning on the Givens case."

"Oh, right. What happened at Quinault?"

"First promise that you won't scream and throw things."

I could feel my mouth set in a tight line. This one would be bad.

Increasingly, the sexual assault cases I assisted with occurred on the Quinault Nation reservation. I never expected to deal with a Native tribe. It happened because of how Ian died, and where. Since his death, and since Jeremy treated me more as a partner than a paralegal, I'd slowly built up trust with members of the tribal council.

And with one nonmember, but Jeremy didn't know about that. Nor did Kyle.

That Native trust in the law firm built so slowly was completely understandable, given the history. It helped that we weren't a government organization. It also helped that tribes needed as much outside aid as they could get, due to the screwed-up jurisdiction laws.

Tribal girls and women were sexually assaulted at rates far higher than other American women, and 86 percent of the assaulters were nontribal. Over decades, the feds decreed that tribes could not prosecute what the government still called "non-Indians" who commited crimes on tribal land. No—they could prosecute sexual crimes, but only if they happened between "intimate partners." No—they couldn't, this was a federal matter. No—it was a state matter. Previous court cases were overturned, laws changed, changed again.

The result was a patchwork of jurisdictional authority depending on who, when, where, and our daily lunch orders. At the moment, tribes had the right to arrest and prosecute in crimes that occurred on tribal land. Off tribal land, if the victim was an enrolled member of the tribe and the perpetrator was not, tribal police could arrest but the state would prosecute, unless the crime is federal. Federal power trumps everybody.

Kidnapping is a federal crime. A U.S. attorney was supposed to prosecute abduction, rape, and missing-women cases (of which there were a heartbreaking number). But there were too few deputies to make arrests and too few prosecutors to bring charges, even when the fuckers could be found. And a lot of prosecutors just didn't bother. Last year, the U.S. Justice Department declined to prosecute 68 percent of rape cases reported on reservations. Many more weren't even reported.

Jeremy said, "Tribal police found a thirteen-year-old girl who'd been kidnapped two days ago. She was unconscious in the national forest, off tribal lands. She'd been raped and beaten. She's in the clinic at Taholah, barely conscious, but she did say the three men who—"

"Three? *Three?*"

"—did this were white. Her grandmother called here, asking for you. The girl's name is Lisa Anderson, her mother is Marina Anderson, and her grandmother is Naomi Patterson. But I'm afraid there's more. The girl's father and two uncles, all of them Ms. Patterson's sons, are out looking for the men, and almost certainly everybody is armed."

"Did you alert U.S. deputies that—"

"Of course I did," he said irritably. "And if any cops—state or tribal or federal—catch the bastards, I'll personally make sure this case gets prosecuted. But right now, you need to get to Taholah and interview the mother, grandmother, and Lisa, if possible. Record everything, if they'll let you. God only knows how long it'll take the feds to get anybody over there. Tell them all that we're prepared to do, and try to secure as much cooperation as they're willing to give. It's a positive that Ms. Patterson wants you and nobody else."

"I'm on my way."

Thirteen years old. Three men.

It was a three-and-a-half-hour drive to the Quinault Nation, located on more than 200,000 acres along the ocean in the world's only temperate-climate rainforest. It is beautiful, remote, wet country. I drove along roads bordered by Sitka spruce, red alder, western hemlock. The air smelled of pine and loam, an earthy, clean smell. A black-tailed deer ran across the road in front of me and I barely missed hitting it. It could have been a black bear or even a cougar. Unlike some Native American reservations, the Quinault Nation's rich land is the same location where their ancestors have lived for centuries, hunting game and fishing the ocean.

The ocean, however, is not the same.

Over the last decade, parts of the village of Taholah, home to 800 people, has been moved a half mile from seaside to higher ground. As the Pacific Ocean rose from global warming and weather became more extreme, storm surges overtopped the seawall and flooded Taholah. The Army Corps of Engineers repaired it twice, but floods became too frequent. The entire village was supposed to be moved, but funds ran out. And, of course, there is the Blob, which no amount of shifting townships will remedy.

Carefully, I drove into Taholah without looking at all at the ocean. I could hear it, smell it, but I couldn't look. Not yet. I needed my whole mind to concentrate on Lisa Anderson.

The Taholah Medical Center was new, bright, and well run. The young woman at the desk, June Barker, waved me toward Lisa's room. Marina and Naomi sat on either side of Lisa's bed. The girl lay asleep, her face swollen and bandaged as no child's should ever be, her arm in a cast.

Marina stared at me flatly, but Naomi, who made the decisions in this family, nodded a dignified welcome. She knew that I saw the pain in her dark eyes, and that I shared it. For Lisa, and for Ian. It made a fragile bond between us.

I asked, "What does the doctor say? Is it Dr. Gooding?" Daniel Gooding, a registered member of the Quinault Nation with a medical degree from UW, was one of the best and most caring doctors I knew.

It was Naomi who answered. "Yes. He says Lisa's body will recover."

She didn't need to add the rest. I took out my recorder, got signed permission, and set to work, fighting to not let fury deter me.

When I left Lisa's room an hour later, she still hadn't wakened from the sedative. Naomi followed me. In the corridor she said quietly, "Joe wants to see you. He's waiting on the beach."

All at once the air left the clinic, and I couldn't breathe.

"Yes," Naomi said. "It's starting again."

2011: SEATTLE, WASHINGTON

JAKE'S MOVIE, *Year of the Goat*, opened to wonderful reviews and great box office. And just like that, Jake was a star. Red carpets, print and radio interviews, David Letterman and Conan O'Brien and Ellen DeGeneres, a *Vanity Fair* profile, tabloid photos. I hated all of it.

YEAR OF THE GOAT CREATES A STAR—JAKE SANDERSON'S METEORIC RISE

CHARACTER ACTORS ARE HOLLYWOOD'S REAL ACTORS: PAUL GIAMATTI, STEVE BUSCEMI, KATHY BATES, AND JAKE SANDERSON

IT'S ALL JAKE

WHAT IS JAKE SANDERSON HIDING? HIS SECRET LIFE EXPOSED!

What Jake was hiding was a wife and son. I refused to be interviewed by anyone, would not let photos be taken of me or Ian (they were anyway, of course, whenever we left the apartment), stayed off social media. Most of all, I refused to move to Los Angeles.

"Renata, I have to be there," Jake said in February. "You know that."

"So be there. I'm not leaving my job, my life here."

"And I respect that." He had on his exaggeratedly patient expression, which always made me want to slap him. "But you knew when you married me that—"

"What I knew when I married you was that you were a fine actor who wanted to do mostly stage. Real acting. You wanted to play Macbeth! And now you just signed for a part in—what is it? The third sequel to something inane to start with?"

"It's a big part," he said, his jaw hard as an erection. "And a lot of money. Which helps pay, incidentally, for this apartment and Ian's nanny."

"Yes," I said, refusing to sound grateful that Jake was supporting his own son.

"You're staying here if I move to L.A.?"

"I am."

"Then I want Ian to stay with me half time."

"No. Absolutely not. He's eighteen months old, for fuck's sake! He belongs with me." Panic edged my voice, even though I knew that Jake wouldn't really try to have Ian half-time in L.A. His life involved too many nights out, too many sudden trips, too much uncertainty.

"The nanny can come with him. I love him, too, Renata!"

"I know. But you can't . . . I can't . . ."

Abruptly Jake softened. "Yes. I know. Only . . . please move with me, Renata. I need you."

"You don't need me," I said, and it almost tore me apart to realize that it was true. We no longer needed each other. The only times we came together without tension were in bed. Sex was still good, if infrequent.

Jake was silent a long time. Then he said quietly, "Maybe I don't."

Words slithered into my mind, slimy and unwelcome: *Let's find out.*

"Mommy!" Ian said, toddling out of his bedroom. "I get out!"

It was the first time he'd climbed out of his crib, and he looked as proud of himself as if he'd scaled Everest.

In 2014, Jake appeared in two movies. One got decent reviews, the other got only 26 percent favorable on Rotten Tomatoes. I didn't see either one of them, or much of Jake. When he came "home" to Seattle, which wasn't often, I left him alone with Ian as much as I could and spent extra time at work. Since I'd started at Stanley, Broome

& Hardwick, I'd gone back to school—Jake paid for that, too—and qualified as a paralegal. I liked that no one at the firm treated me any differently because I was Jake Sanderson's wife. On paper, I was paralegal to Jeremy Hardwick, but the job had grown to include much more than that. I did organize Jeremy, who desperately needed it; entropy enveloped him like fog on Elliott Bay. But I also accompanied him on depositions for his pro bono work on sexual assault, and I made the discovery that I was better at bonding with the confused and frightened victims, many very young, than even the firm's female lawyers. The work was heartbreaking and deeply satisfying, in about equal measure.

In supermarket checkout lines, I sometimes saw photos of Jake with actresses, right next to headlines like SECRET ALIEN STRONGHOLD ON THE MOON! I didn't know what Jake's relationships were to these women, and I didn't ask. We never slept together anymore. Jake paid the bills and saw Ian whenever he could, and if I sometimes lay awake at night wondering how he could be so different from the man I married—how we could be so different together—at daybreak I pushed the thoughts away and got on with it.

Then Dylan drove up to Seattle to see me.

Twenty minutes of chit-chat, mostly about Dylan's life in Portland. He wanted to make detective, but it wasn't happening. According to him, his superiors, right up to the commissioner, had an unreasonable and unfounded grudge against Dylan. This didn't seem likely to me, but I said nothing.

He drained his coffee and said abruptly, "You haven't asked about Jake."

I didn't see why I would ask Dylan about Jake.

He said, "I saw him recently. Went down there to surprise him. He barely had time for me."

"Well . . . isn't he shooting a TV show or something?"

"Renata—you're defending him? You? After the way he's treated you?"

"I wasn't defending him." Was I?

"He's forgotten you, me, even Ian. He thinks he's too big for us now."

"I don't think that's true, Dylan. It's just that—"

"You wouldn't be defending him if you knew what I know."

A wave of queasiness roiled through me. I knew, even before Dylan said it. I'd known for a long time. What I hadn't known, hadn't realized, was how jealous Dylan was of Jake, that he would do what he was going to do.

Dylan said, "Jake is having an affair."

"I know," I said.

"You do?"

"Yes. Dylan, why did you tell me?"

But he couldn't bear to go there. I could barely go there myself. At the same time, I had to admit this was at least in part my fault. I had pushed Jake away, again and again. He was needy, successful, rich, and, if not exactly handsome, enormously appealing. Of course there was a woman. Or women.

Dylan said, sulky now, "Her name is Kitra Jordan. She's an actress."

"Yes," I said. "I'm going now, Dylan. I'm not angry with you—" he was too pathetic to be angry with "—but I'm going." I walked out of the coffee shop.

The worst thing was that Jake and I didn't fight about Kitra Jordan. The fire had gone out of us, at least with regard to each other. Perhaps because we both recognized our culpability, the divorce was quiet and non-acrimonious. Washington is a community property state. I got half of everything Jake had earned. I put most of it away for Ian and kept on working at the law firm.

More years, more movies, more responsibility at work. Jake broke up with Kitra and took up with someone else, then someone after that. He was nominated for an Oscar for Best Supporting Actor and lost. A few years later, he won. Donald Trump was elected president. Four years later, he wasn't. Ian discovered chess, and I spent Monday nights driving him to weekly matches at a local club, where he mainlined Skittles between moves against much older players. Often he won. My hair started to gray, and I decided against dying it.

And then, all at once, nobody's thoughts in the entire nation were on anything but the Catastrophe, as the economy crashed, and entire companies too big to fail nonetheless went into bankruptcy, and people died, all brought down by a single letter of the alphabet.

2022: INDIA

THE CATASTROPHE broke while Ian and I were in India.

He had spent the two-week winter vacation from school, which somehow got extended to nearly another week, with Jake in Los Angeles. Three weeks in which I missed him and worried about him and enjoyed the guilty freedom of being alone. No babysitters, no arguments about whether an eleven-year-old needed a babysitter, no driving him to chess matches and friends' houses and school events. No arguments about whether an eleven-year-old should take buses alone, or climb out on the roof to view a meteor shower, or have his Facebook page monitored. But at the airport he kissed me good bye, and for those three weeks, I clung to phone calls and memories and plans for when Ian returned to Seattle.

He left an eleven-year-old nerd, dressed in

Levi's, a tee that said CHESS PLAYERS HAVE GREAT MOVES, and a baseball cap. He returned looking like a thirty-two-year-old investment banker trying to be cool, dressed in a $300 Ferragamo zip-front polo, designer jeans, and sockless shoes that cost more than my weekly salary. He carried a state-of-the-art laptop that could probably have moved satellites in orbit. Jake had invested in an independent production company that had struck movie gold with two wildly popular films about aliens who battled Earth. Jake was rich.

"Wow, look at you," I said, not approvingly.

Ian could always read me. "You don't like it. Dad said you wouldn't. But just because some of the world isn't blessed doesn't mean that we shouldn't enjoy the fact that through our own efforts, we are."

I stared at him. No way that was Ian talking, or even Jake. I asked, "Who is she?"

"Who's who?" But he shifted from one foot to the other as we faced each other at the SeaTac arrival gate. Passengers streamed past.

"Your dad's new girlfriend. It's okay, Ian, he's an adult. So am I."

He turned sulky. "Sage Scott."

I blinked. She was a huge international star with more beauty than talent. "Well," I said heartily, "that's fine. But—"

"Mom," Ian blurted out, "don't hassle me because I like money, okay?"

"Money is useful," I said, and hugged him again.

But it wasn't that easy. With almost-teenagers, it never is. There were times during the next week when I wanted to apologize to my long-dead parents for my own teen years.

Ian was disdainful of his old school and wanted to transfer to one that had a good lacrosse team.

Ian was disdainful of his old clothes.

Ian refused to go with me to the soup kitchen where once a week for years now, we'd helped feed the homeless.

When Ian said, "People can always feed themselves if they just try, just like the rest of the world could if it got its act together. All you have to do is grow food," I'd had enough. Arguments weren't going to do it here. He needed immersion learning.

"Pack up your designer duds," I said. "We're taking a field trip."

"Where?"

"Overseas."

"I don't want to. Mom, I missed enough school already."

"Like you really mind that. And we'll only be gone for a long weekend, so pack up."

He was eleven, and eleven-year-olds don't have

household veto. Not in my house. Ian went with me. Sulky, barricaded during the long flight behind laptop and earbuds and resentment, he went.

Chennai was a huge, prosperous commercial and cultural center in southern India. A tourist draw, it had the gorgeous Kapaleeswarar Temple, museums, parks, a British fort dating from the Raj, the Tamil film industry. That was not the Chennai I took Ian to.

I'd arranged for a guide who, along with an armed bodyguard, took us to outlying slums, to coastal villages flooded by the rising sea, to fields so ravaged by inland drought or coastal salt water that they could grow nothing. Ian saw ragged, starving children living in tin boxes, beggars whose bones stuck out sharp as chisels, a fight over the food on an aid truck that left two people lying bloody in the road. Each night I brought him back to Chennai to eat rich food in expensive restaurants. I spent the money from my divorce freely, and I didn't have to say a word.

Sweating in the heat, Ian said, "Sage was wrong. Those people—they can't grow enough food."

"No. Each year, childhood deaths from malnutrition rise sharply, and it's only going to get worse. The need for food is projected to rise 70 percent over the next thirty years. And as to poverty—well, a handful of super-rich people have as much money as the whole bottom half of the world's population put together."

"That can't be right?"

"It's not right."

"I mean, that can't be *correct*."

"It is."

He said nothing more, staring at a child digging through a stinking garbage dump for something to eat. Back at the hotel, after a shower, I saw him checking statistics on his laptop. At dinner he stared at the exquisitely cooked food on his plate.

"Mom, what can we do?"

"Donate. Understand the situation. Care."

He picked up his fork, put it down again, scowled. But not, this time, at me. I thought I saw down beginning on his upper lip—could that be true? So soon?

"I can sell a lot of my stuff," Ian said, "and donate the money."

"That's your choice, honey," I said. "But keep what you really need. The trick is to decide what that is."

He nodded. I thought, *Take that, Sage.*

But I knew I was really talking to Jake.

Our Air India flight landed at JFK to utter bed-lam. At first I thought it was a terrorist attack. But Ian, glued to his phone as we walked through the jetway, said, "Mom, a lot of kids died from pills."

"Pills? What pills? A contaminated street drug? Or overdoses? I've warned you time and again that—"

"No. Look!" He thrust his phone at me, but by then we were off the jetway and a TV blared at us, volume loud, people buzzing around it like angry gnats.

". . . another sixteen children dead in three states—"

". . . and if you or your family have any of this product in your home, do not use it! Don't flush it into the water system or put it in the garbage. Take it to your doctor's office or the closest ER, where it will be destroyed in a way that does not contaminate the environment. To repeat this im-portant warning—"

"As panic spreads—"

"Mom," Ian said again, and now he sounded scared.

"Come on, honey," I said. "It'll be all right. Let's get an Uber home."

Even then, I knew it was not all right. But not I, not anyone, understood the full weight of what was to come.

It turns out that it takes only a few months to destroy an entire national economy.

It wasn't really a few months, of course. This had been simmering a long time. But it might have gone on simmering if it weren't for Klenbar, an antidiarrhea drug manufactured by agribusiness giant Meridian Enterprises. Meridian, along with three other agribusiness companies, grows 80 percent of America's food, including corn, soybeans, wheat, and sugar beet. All except the wheat contain genetically modified organisms. So did Klenbar.

The drug was biopharmed: made from genetically altered plants grown on a heavily fenced farm in Indiana. It had FDA approval and had been on the market for two years with no problems. During development, Klenbar had been tested and tested again. Since then, hundreds of thousands of moms had given it to children to prevent dehydration during childhood illnesses. It worked well, tasted good, and had no side effects.

Then something went wrong and, before Klenbar was identified as the cause, a hundred sixteen children in thirty states died.

Later, scientists would figure out what had happened. It was a "monkey event"—if enough monkeys type long enough, eventually they will produce *Hamlet* even though the odds are vanishingly small. Minuscule odds are not zero odds. The Klenbar monkey event happened through horizontal gene transfer: the movement of genetic material between unrelated species by some means other than reproduction. With Klenbar, the means was *Agrobacteria tumefaciens*, a bacterium that occurs naturally in soil. Genetic engineers often use *A. tumefaciens,* custom modified, to introduce new genes into plants.

Bacteria are promiscuous. They are constantly exchanging genes with each other and the environment. The Klenbar tragedy occurred because a bacterium picked up a lethal gene from a soil fungus that should not have been there and transferred it to the GMO plant growing a key ingredient of the drug. The usual antibiotic cleansing of *A. tumefaciens* from the harvested plant missed the fungus gene, which nobody was looking for. Genes express only under certain conditions; the lethal gene found those conditions. The entire chain of events was a millions-to-one chance occurrence.

But it had happened.

Gene expression is complicated by so many factors: epigenetics, micro-RNAs, environmental conditions. Risk assessment is even more complicated, and most people do it very badly. Ask 100 people on an ocean beach whether they are more likely to die from a shark attack or from a bath in their own bathtub, and ninety-nine of them will get it wrong.

The GMO debate had been simmering for decades. Pro-GMO people pointed out the equivalence of GMO food to "natural" crops, which weren't natural at all due to extensive cross-breeding, and to the need to feed the world. They declared those who opposed genetic engineering to be antiscience, Luddites, unhumanitarian. Anti-GMO people pointed to the risks of monoculture failure, heavy use of pesticides, and unpredictable changes to ecosystems. They declared the opposition to be reckless, tools of agribusiness, and unhumanitarian.

Both sides were right, although the problem so far had never been the GMOs themselves but the way they were used. Instead of improving the food supply for the needy developing world, agribusinesses concentrated on profitable crops for richer nations. They fought hard to resist giving information to consumers, including labeling food and explaining what heavy chemicals were being sprayed on fields that sometimes abutted residential areas. Agribusinesses were right, however, when they'd insisted that no person anywhere had ever been harmed by any GMO.

Until now.

I spent hours staring at the TV. Protests across the country escalated into violence, flames, and shooting.

SAY NO TO GMO!

GMO = DEAD KIDS

CLEAN FOOD FOR OUR KIDS

Meridian had immediately recalled all bottles of Klenbar. But people—a lot of people—didn't get the word. They gave Klenbar to their sick children, and those children died.

KILL THE GMO KILLERS!

LOCK THEM ALL UP!

Some lunatic with an illegal assault rifle fired on Meridian employees reporting for work at the company's manufacturing facility. The shooter fired during a shift change and twelve people died, including three of the protestors beside the front gates. An off-duty cop shot the killer, and then someone in the crowd shot the cop.

A fringe ecoterrorist group deliberately injected poison into cardboard bottles of coffee creamer in a supermarket in Chicago. More people died. The coffee creamer was made of soy; 90 percent of soybeans grown in the United States are genetically engineered. A huge number of planted social-media posts declared that the GMO soy had killed and that the government and agribusinesses were conspiring to cover it up.

Greenpeace, which had always ripped up fields

of GMO crops by night, sometimes while wearing theatrical hazmat suits or gas masks, now did so openly. The theatrics were still present, however, along with plenty of news drones.

The protests did not slacken. Demonstrations began to target lawmakers, especially those up for reelection in November. Candidates opposing them sprang up, some legitimate but some promising everything from a total ban on GMOs to burning the CEO of Meridian Enterprises as the Antichrist.

Agricultural commodity markets had always been highly volatile in economic terms, but not like this. The stock market plunged, rallied, and then, after the soy poisonings, dragged the entire country into a depression. People tried to grow their own food in backyards, on decks, on rooftops. Organic farms sold out of produce as people hoarded. Hoarding caused more riots. Meridian declared bankruptcy. It looked as if, without a bailout, Monsanto and Dow might do the same. The unemployment rate soared. The violence continued.

I didn't care about any of it. Not after May 6, 2022.

"I can beat him, Mom. I know I can. I've been studying!" Ian bent over his suitcase, packing his chess clock. He was spending the weekend on the Quinault reservation, a first for us. Chess prodigies can spring up anywhere, and Lawrence Underwood had a father willing to drive him all around the Northwest for tournaments. Lawrence, a year older than Ian, was the better player, but that only seemed to spur Ian on. The boys had liked each other immediately and over the last year had become friends. It seemed to me that Lawrence's father was not thrilled about the friendship. However, Ian had been invited to go home with Lawrence for the weekend after a tournament in Aberdeen.

I drove him there, hearing Ian chatter about chess in the way that all mothers learn to do: listening without actually listening. I registered the rise and fall of his voice, the pitch and inflections and pauses that let me interject an appropriate "Really!" or "Then what?" I wasn't absorbing information about chess; I was absorbing the excitement of my sweet boy.

He lost his match; Lawrence won his. Ian called me Saturday afternoon. "Mom, we're going clamming and Mrs. Underwood says I have to get your permission. Can I please go? Please?"

"Sure. And remember to thank your hosts for taking you." It was the very end of the season, and the clams had been particularly juicy that year.

"I will! Bye! Love you!"

What did I do the rest of that day? I can't remember. Nothing is clear until the second phone call, Sunday morning. "Mrs. Sanderson," said a quiet female voice that didn't know I'd dropped Jake's surname, "this is Naomi Patterson. I am Lawrence's grandmother. Ian and Lawrence and some other children are in the Taholah Medical Center, very sick. It might be bad clams."

The world stopped. When it started up again, it reverberated with one thunderous sound: *No*.

Did I say good bye to Naomi? I can't remember. All I remember is that roaring *No*, and the Blob floating off the coast, an unseasonably early algae bloom. And then the birds.

As I sped along the coast, a bird dove at my car, hitting the windshield in a spatter of feathers and blood. It slid off the hood as another darted this way and that before falling out of the sky. It landed, flapping wings on the ground.

Then I knew for sure.

This had happened before.

The Blob—all the blobs—was caused by a stable high-pressure region in the atmosphere. Winds hadn't mixed the cooler water under the ocean's surface with the warmer water at the surface, which had just gone on getting warmer and warmer in the sunshine. April temperatures had averaged fifteen degrees above normal. The main algae out there in the bloom, *Pseudo-nitzschia*, loved it. Nothing else did. *P-nitzschia* outcompeted most other microscopic marine life.

Under the right circumstances, *P-nitzschia* manufactured domoic acid, a neurotoxin. The algae didn't always make the toxin; "the right circumstances" included the presence of certain marine bacteria. *P-nitzschia* was a major food for tiny sea creatures that then were eaten by shellfish, razor clams, sardines, anchovies, small fish. Most of those experience no ill effects. Not so for the birds that eat them. Domoic acid, the structural analog of glutamate, causes excitotoxity. With enough domoic acid, bird brains overload. The crazed birds lose all sense of direction, swooping and diving psychotically, crashing into things. Sometimes they die.

So do otters, sea lions, larger mammals.

In 1961, birds that had ingested domoic acid went crazy in a California beach town. Alfred Hitchcock made a movie about it.

In 1987, three people on Prince Edward Island, Canada, died from eating blue mussels laden with domoic acid. Neither cooking nor freezing affects the toxin. There is no antidote.

In 2004, a bloom with *P-nitzschia* toxins closed beaches the entire summer, destroying razor-clam harvests and crab fisheries.

In 2020, six people in Florida died from eating toxin-laden sardines.

The bloom I tore past now had been certified as not producing domoic acid. But the Catastrophe had just happened, and, it turned out, certification hadn't been updated. The Washington Departments of Health and of Fish and Wildlife had their hands full. National Oceanic and Atmospheric Administration and the U.S. Integrated Observing System were struggling to survive. People assumed the beaches were safe because no one told them otherwise. Unsafe ingestion of domoic acid occurs at 20 milligrams per kilo of body weight.

Sometime during Saturday night, Ian and Lawrence and five other people began to vomit.

Then cramps and diarrhea, fouling beds.

Then dizziness, confusion, mucus from the nose.

Then seizures and cardiac arrhythmias as the neurotoxin burned out all muscular control.

For five of those people, things didn't progress that far. They had more body weight, they preferred other foods with their clams, they were not a slight, nerdy eleven-year-old who loved clams above all other foods. I sat beside his bed, holding his hand, talking to him even though he didn't answer. The copter was on its way to airlift him to a bigger hospital. It would be all right; it had to be all right.

The copter was delayed. The arrythmia caused by the excitatory toxin could not be controlled.

I was still holding Ian's hand when he stopped breathing.

Jake, without Sage Scott, flew up from L.A. for Ian's funeral. I don't remember much about it. Nothing really penetrated through my fog of grief, rage, and sedatives. The aftermath is what I remember more clearly, when Jake had gone back to his life. The terrible flowers (white for the death of a child) thrown on a compost heap. The people who had been solicitous reabsorbed into the national Catastrophe. It was the aftermath that remains as clear in my mind as a knife in my brain.

I walked the beach where Ian died, every day for the rest of that summer. The beach was on tribal land and I must have been observed, but no one stopped me. I stared at the algae bloom on the ocean until I thought I would go blind. I cursed and yelled. The one thing I could not do was cry. That seemed monstrous to me, that I could not cry for Ian. I was stone: not the cold rigid stone of boulders but the furious, erupting rock of volcanoes. Jeremy, when he could not get me to do my job, gave me a paid leave of absence.

At night, I drank at my unwashed kitchen table, with an index card propped up against the bottle in front of me. On the index card, I'd drawn a diagram copied from the internet:

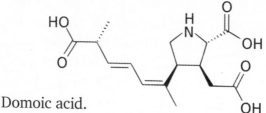

Domoic acid.

I drank more, and barely left my apartment until, one night, my doorbell rang over and over. When I could no longer stand the clanging in my head, I flung open the door, ready to scream at whoever stood there.

It was a small, old woman, a young and muscular man hovering protectively behind. "I'm Naomi Patterson," she said in the voice I remembered from that terrible phone call. "You have to stop now."

"Stop walking the beach because it's on tribal land? I won't stop. No." I was ready to fight—her, him, the world.

"You can walk on the beach if you choose to. But you have to stop destroying yourself."

The sheer effrontery of this fueled my rage. "Who are you to—"

"It's who *you* are that matters. I need you."

"You . . . need me? What the fuck are you talking about?"

"I saw you in court with the other lawyer for my niece, Elizabeth Brown."

I remembered Elizabeth Brown. She had been assaulted by a non-Native, and Jeremy had worked with the state prosecutor trying the attacker. Jeremy had, in fact, done nearly all the work except the actual litigation; Elizabeth Brown had not been a priority for the overworked D.A. I'd helped prepare Elizabeth, traumatized, to testify. She'd had family with her, silent and suspicious. Maybe one of them had been Naomi. Tribal members don't like accepting our help, even when they can benefit from it. But there are not enough Native lawyers to go around.

She said, "Another Quinault woman has been accused of a crime she didn't commit. I need you and your lawyer." She said it as if I were Jeremy's boss, not the other way around. "Your son and my great-grandson were friends. Your son died with us. You must help us."

I didn't follow her logic, and I don't think the man beside her did, either. He continued to stare at me impassively, a stocky young man dressed in jeans and a plain tee, with his black hair in a man bun. I didn't know until later that he was another of Naomi's grandchildren, and that he and she were two of the three people who would lift me out of the abyss and back to life.

The third person, an even more improbable savior, was Dylan Sanderson.

2022: SEATTLE

THE MID-TERM ELECTIONS following the Catastrophe caused the greatest turnover of power in American history. Lawmakers who had supported GMOs, or had ties with agribusiness, or were suspected of somehow being complicit in something lost their seats at both federal and state levels. Not all of them, of course, but enough to change everything.

Until the Catastrophe, the battle versus GMO crops had been a battle against uncertainty: what might they do to health, environment, biodiversity? After the Catastrophe, uncertainty was gone, at least in the minds of 65 percent of the public, as determined by multiple polls. Expensive and vigorous PR campaigns did not change many minds. Genetic engineering was Satan. It had brought Armageddon. This was a holy war.

All GM crops were banned from farms in the

United States. The EU, which had banned growing and importing GMOs twenty-five years earlier, was smug. Also hungry, as U.S. imports disappeared. America was having trouble feeding itself, let alone anybody else.

Prices of organic crops soared. So did organic planting; it was spring. The remaining agribusinesses scrambled to convert to non-GMOs. That didn't change the huge amounts of pesticides, herbicides, and fungicides sprayed on crops, but nobody was looking at that. During a holy war, you concentrate only on the infidels.

The Department of Agricultural Security, DAS, was created to enforce the ban on GMOs.

None of this was simple. Gene flow always happened between wild and cultivated crops as pollen was borne on the wind. Before the Catastrophe, genes from GMO canola had turned up in wild mustard plants, that tough and pesky roadside weed. Now those genes blew back onto non-GMO canola plants, "contaminating" them. It's hard to put genies back into bottles.

And a lot of people didn't want to.

I talked Jeremy into taking Naomi's great-niece's cousin's case, even though it was not the sort of case he usually handled and the young woman, contrary to Naomi's belief, was guilty of the burglary she was accused of. However, the police had performed so many illegal and racist actions in arresting, searching, and interrogating her that Jeremy had no trouble getting the case dismissed. More cases came to us from the Quinault Nation; evidently Naomi wielded considerable power there. Jeremy made clear that his pro bono work concerned only those situations involving sexual assault. The victims always asked for me. The work did not fill the void—nothing would ever do that—but it filled my days.

Even after my Ian was gone, Dylan would drive from Portland every few months or so to have dinner with me. He missed Ian, too. Although Dylan was far too self-absorbed to fill the father role that Jake had taken on only between movies, Dylan had liked to play video games with Ian and to take him fishing. Dylan was thirty now. He'd been briefly married and acrimoniously divorced, no kids. He still fidgeted.

In January 2024, as we drank coffee in my apartment, he said abruptly, "Jake was offered a part in an anti-GMO movie."

"He was?" I couldn't picture such a film, and then, sickeningly, I could. Evil scientists out to destroy the world, heroic DAS agents, somewhere a scantily clad female informant. Give me a break.

"Jake turned it down."

"Good for him."

"He is in favor of GMOs."

Unless Jake had become an entirely different

person, I already knew that. Dylan watched me intently—why? Finally he said, "I am, too."

"So am I."

"I know. You always were." He drained his coffee, set down the cup and fiddled with the handle, looked straight at me. "Look, Renata, I'm worried about you. You and Jake were the only family I have. You need . . . something. I don't know what. But I know about this group, they're trying to work on GMOs again, this time the way they should have been done in the first place. I wish I could join them, but I can't, and I thought—"

"Of course you can't," I said as startled by that idea as by the notion that I was still family to Dylan. "You're *law enforcement*. Your job is to arrest those people."

He got the mulish look I remembered from his teenage years. "Yeah, well, law enforcement isn't everything that outsiders think it is. There's a lot of stuff about it that I don't like. And that's federal, anyway, not state. But I know I can't join this group, not even to stick it to my captain, and if you're not interested, forget about it. It was just an idea because I'm worried about you. Well, I know about this other group, completely out in the open, that's working on all the homelessness from automation, you could—"

"No," I said, because there were always groups

working to slow down automation, and none of them ever got anywhere. "Tell me about the pro-GMO group." *Ian, saying that Sage was wrong. "Those people—they can't grow enough food. I can sell a lot of my stuff."*

"You can't ever tell this group that you heard about it from me. I'd get in a lot of trouble."

"I won't. I won't involve you at all. Just tell me how to make contact."

Joining the Org wasn't easy. The group was grass-roots, beginning slowly at first and then building fast with a surprising amount of hidden, illegal support from rich donors. Its goal was to rebuild the genetic engineering of crops so that, instead of enriching big agribusinesses, they could save children from hunger and malnutrition. I hung on to Ian's words as an anchor to sanity.

There were probably other groups doing the same thing, but I didn't hear about them—then or ever—because secrecy was so essential. I passed through three layers of recruiters in three different cities, none of whom I ever saw again. DAS was not yet operational, so at least they knew I wasn't a government infiltrator. My background was thoroughly checked, my motives examined. "We don't take people just because they're mad at the world. Or even at a section of the world. How mad are you, Renata, and at whom?"

I told the recruiters about Ian. I told them about Jake, which nearly disqualified me; the spouse of a world-famous movie star might be too visible. Careful research convinced them I was no longer part of Jake's life.

I prepared for my recruitment interviews as thoroughly as I prepared briefs for Jeremy, and I told them nothing but truth: I believed the promise of biotech had been hijacked by corporations who'd bought up patents, processes, and whole companies to focus on profit, not people in need. I knew how much the global demand for food would rise in coming decades, and how much more woodland and rain forest would have to be cleared to meet it, further accelerating climate change. And I asked the important question: how can you be sure the genemod crops you create won't replicate the Klenbar disaster? They had the right answers, including information on new gene-editing techniques that didn't involve using bacteria or viruses as intermediaries to change DNA.

They were, the recruiters said in nonspecific terms, working to develop varied crops that would grow in acidic soils; 43 percent of tropical soils are acidic. That would grow in drought conditions; creeping desertification was projected for the next forty years. That would be more resistant to pests and diseases without such heavy use of sprayed chemicals. That would increase yields or nutritional benefits.

They took me. Between my work for the Org and my work with the Quinault Nation, my life once again acquired focus and meaning. The aching hollow where Ian had been would never fill, and my nights were still bad. It might have helped if I had been able to cry, but I never could. Some nights it felt like the pent-up tears would crush me with the weight of unshed water. But I was at least functional.

And then, on the beach where Ian died, I met Joe Peck again.

It had been months since I'd been back to the beach. But all at once, after a meeting in Taholah, I wanted to see the Pacific when the Blob wasn't sitting offshore and the water was blue and glistening. There wasn't much actual beach to see; the tide was in and loose logs were drifting almost to the bluff. A man stooped at the water's edge, filling vials.

Anyone who filled vials with sea water was either a techie or a lunatic. No one else was around, but I had my gun in my pocket, and I ignored the man. He straightened as I passed and gave me a look I knew well from Taholah: absolutely opaque courtesy. I was there, he acknowledged I was there, interaction between us was not going to happen.

The beach was dotted with the tiny dimples that indicated razor clams below the surface of the sand. I stared at them, unable to look away. A sudden large wave jumped from the sea and soaked my shoes and pants.

"Fuck!" I said. The North Pacific is stingingly cold. I bent to take off my water-filled shoes.

All at once the man said, "I know you."

"I don't think so." I straightened quickly and faced him, my hand on the Beretta in my jacket pocket. But he made no move toward me. Instead he stared at my wrist. The sleeve of my jacket had ridden up when I bent over, exposing the bracelet of ugly, Tiffany Teal plastic. I'd forgotten to take it off since the morning's Org meeting. My neck prickled—did he know something? Was he DAS or some other federal agency?

"You're Renata Black," he said. "You worked with the attorney who defended my cousin in U.S. court. Elizabeth Brown."

The case that Naomi had insisted I take, showing up at my door with . . . yes, this man. I recognized him now.

He said, "I'm Joe Peck."

"Yes," I said. "Bye." I didn't want to talk to him, to know him. He'd seen my bracelet and stared at it like he knew what it meant. He knew my real name. He could connect my two lives. Not good.

But he said, "I'm with NOAA. We track *P-nitzschia*."

"I hope you're better at it now than you were two years ago."

"We are. But that's not all I do. Gorgeous view, isn't it?"

I stared at him. Did he mean . . .

I responded, "I always find looking at this so calming," and we went through the whole inane conversation that Org members use to identify each other.

"Why did you do that, Joe?"

"I realized that you saw me recognize your bracelet. You're at Taholah a lot, with your real name. I didn't want you worrying I'm DAS or reporting this to your cell. We're not supposed to know each other."

"No."

"Don't wear your bracelet here," he said, unsmiling. It was clearly an order, something I would ordinarily resent, but he was right. Then he added another order. "And get someplace warm to get out of those wet clothes. The water temperature is forty-six Fahrenheit."

"Okay. But, Joe—will you do something for me?"

"Probably not."

"Please. If the algae starts producing domoic acid again . . . will you tell me? As Renata Black, from a NOAA employee? Nothing to do with the Org."

I don't know what my face showed, how much naked need. Whatever it was, or for some reason of his own, Joe agreed.

The Blob formed on the water that summer but did not produce toxin. The country was still in economic chaos from the Catastrophe. I looked up NOAA on the internet; its website detailed the reductions in staff and activities that had been made as funding was cut by Congress. The Washington State Department of Fish and Wildlife was the only one monitoring *P-nitzschia*.

I resumed visiting the beach. Whenever Joe was there, he talked about algae blooms, telling me things I already knew from the internet. Fifty percent of the fertilizer used on crops was not taken up by plants, was washed into the watershed, and ended up in the ocean, where its nutrients fed lush blooms. Did that mean the Org was working on crops that would not need so much fertilizer, that might, for instance, be able to fix their own nitrogen from the air or soil? I didn't ask. He wouldn't have told me, not even if he knew.

I kept going to the beach, making the long drive three or four times a week, all that summer and then even after the autumn rains had started.

Eventually, from my persistence or his compassion, and undoubtedly with permission from higher in the Org, he told me what his cell was actually trying to accomplish, and for the first time since Ian's death five years ago, I broke down and cried.

2032: SEATTLE, WASHINGTON

TWO DAYS after Lisa Anderson had been found in the woods, I called Naomi from my apartment in Seattle. Lisa was being discharged from the clinic and was doing as well as could be expected. Naomi's sons had not found Lisa's attackers. I was grateful for that, and I think Naomi was, too. She didn't need any more of her family ensnared in the United States justice system, and certainly not as indicted murderers.

Today, a Saturday, I had two stations to visit, not too far apart. At a Keep It Safe!, I changed from Renata Black to Caroline Denton. Tom was not with me; for the time being, he would know the location of only the carrot station. Kyle was being his usual cautious self.

Miles later, I parked my car in the lot of a supermarket and walked along increasingly rural roads, wearing a sunhat with a wide brim, until I reached an isolated farmhouse with an attached greenhouse.

Jamie Chuchua met me at the door. "Caro. You just caught me."

"Hey, Jamie. Just a routine check to see what's going on with the teff."

Her face lit up. Jamie was sixty-nine, white-haired, and beautiful as I will never be. Perfect bone structure and huge expressive eyes, both attributes that lasted. She was chief for this station, a geneticist passionately committed to teff.

She said, "Come on back and I'll show you. Ben has done wonderful things since you were here last."

We walked through the spacious farmhouse kitchen—pointlessly spacious since only Jamie lived here. Ben and Tessa, also geneticists, lived and worked elsewhere and donated assistance here part time. Jamie and I passed into the greenhouse. Immediately I could feel my skin tighten. It must have been over a hundred degrees, with zero humidity. The earth in the raised planting beds was gray and cracked, the plants in them withered. The greenhouse was a drought-ridden corner of Ethiopia.

Or a preview of what parts of Eastern Washington were becoming. And, presumably, the Midwest could become in the future.

"Look." Jamie pointed at a bed in the back. Its

soil was just as cracked and sere as the others, but green shoots pushed toward the sunlit roof.

Jamie said, "Grown with *half* the water that produced the plants in that bed to the left, and just as healthy. So far, anyway."

The plants looked like foot-high, pale-green grasses, each tipped with tiny grains of teff. In Ethiopia and Eritrea, a third of all arable land grows teff, which can survive droughts that are not too severe, even when the soil is so dry that it heaves and splits, stressing plant roots. Jamie's station was engineering teff for conditions even drier than that.

She said, "Caro, we're down to a projected 100 millimeters of water. If Ben and I—but this is mostly Ben's work—can keep it at that, or even at 150, we're home!"

Teff needs a minimum of 250 millimeters of water during its growth cycle. Dropping that number to 100 millimeters would enable hundreds of thousands of people to survive famine. I said, "That's wonderful."

"It is!" Jamie's face looked as if she'd swallowed the sun. "You'll have a good report to take back to Kyle. But there's more. This variety should, if all the engineering works, have bigger seeds, meaning more nutritional yield per plant. Oh, and come into the kitchen to taste the newest dish."

I trailed behind her, glad to escape the heat of the greenhouse but unwilling to taste the new dish. I don't like teff. It's a valuable food: nourishing, nutty, versatile. You can use it to make porridge, muffins, a spongy and fermented bread called injera, an alcoholic beverage. It's gluten-free, protein-rich, and not susceptible to the mycotoxins that afflict many African staple crops. I still don't like it. It tastes like sawdust to me. Nutty and nutritious sawdust.

"This is a teff pudding," Jamie said, taking a small dish out of the fridge. "Go ahead, taste."

I did. "I taste maple syrup." Maple-favored sawdust. "A lot of maple syrup in Ethiopia, is there?"

"That one's for the potential American market," said a deep masculine voice. Ben stood in the doorway, grinning. Originally from Ethiopia, he still had a slight accent and was one of the handsomest men I ever met.

"Well, some people might like it," I said, putting the pudding dish on the counter.

Ben laughed. "I admire your honesty, Caro. You never soft-pedal anything."

Jake's voice in my head: Can't you ever pick tact over honesty?

Jamie said, "Fortunately, 'some people' do like teff. Me, for instance."

"You're doing great here, Ben, Jamie. Kyle will be thrilled."

Jamie said, "How could you tell? He always looks like he's tasting lemons." She was slightly pissed that I wasn't more enthusiastic about the pudding.

I collected their data cubes and started the long trudge back to my car. Clouds gathered overhead. *Let it rain*, I prayed to gods I didn't believe in. Please let it rain. *It's starting again*, Naomi had said last night. All this summer, the Blob had lain off the coast, green and black in the sunlight, killing everything underneath it. Now, it was beginning to produce domoic acid. The beaches would be closed, but that would not prevent the deaths of pelicans, sooty shearwaters, otters, sea lions. *P-nitzschia* had even killed whales. Rain would dissolve the Blob.

The second station I visited was modifying intermediate wheatgrass, a grain originally from Iran. This work was aimed straight at the United States. All those amber waves of grain of conventional wheat were annuals, with shallow roots that in times of drought—and the plains states were having much more frequent droughts— could neither reach water nor hold the soil against dust storms. Intermediate wheatgrass is a perennial, with a deep root system. It doesn't need to be replanted each year. The seeds are nutritious, but too small, with a yield only half that of domestic wheat. The Org was trying to engineer the plant for both bigger seeds and a higher yield. I picked up the station's report.

Back at the Keep It Safe!, I switched phones and IDs and took out my Contexts. No messages on the Renata phone from Naomi or Joe. As I went to turn off the Caroline phone, it rang.

I stared at it. This phone was only supposed to be used if I found emergency conditions at the teff station. It shouldn't ring. Cell phone conversations were way too easy to hack.

The number was the carrot station in Eastern Washington. My fingers shook. "Hello?"

"They're hitting us now!" Jean Cathcart said. "Don't come, tell Kyle—get away, you! Don't touch me! Don't you—" The connection broke.

I followed procedures. I took the phone into the parking lot, removed the data card, and dissolved it in the jar of acid in the glove compartment. I tossed the empty shell into a dumpster and drove quickly, but not so quickly as to attract attention, back to Seattle. I had to tell Kyle. I was the carrot-station liaison, and Kyle had no traceable connection to the station except through me or Jonas. This was why we were organized the way we were.

Who had hit the carrot station? The feds, the state, a misguided eco-group, a band of lunatic-fringe haters? I hoped it was DAS. That way, Louis and Jean and Miguel would at least be physically intact, under arrest but alive. The same hadn't been always true for Org members taken by haters.

But the station was gone. Whoever had raided it would destroy the greenhouses, the carrots, the years of work to create safe, fruitful crops to feed a developing world that needed them and a developed world that, if global warming continued to accelerate, was going to need them sooner than it thought. I saw again the rows of Danvers carrots that could grow in salty water, in drought, in the Org's hopeful dreams.

Driving back to Seattle, I brought up the news on my dashboard screen. Internet news was often contradictory, slanted, and stunningly inaccurate. But there was nothing about the attack on the station.

From sources of his own, Kyle had already heard. We stood in the side yard, pretending to admire Susan's roses, as I told him exactly what Jean had said. He nodded. "It was DAS."

I said, "Better than if it weren't."

"Yes. RightNews leaked video footage of the arrests. The FBI has surrounded the station, wearing hazmat suits."

"Christ, it's carrots, not weaponized anthrax!"

"To be fair, DAS doesn't know that. But there's something else. I don't know if it's true, but a DAS spokesperson said they found the farm due to a tip received anonymously on their hotline."

I went cold. "That could mean anything. A nosy neighbor, a suspicious relative—"

"I don't think so. The spokesperson gave quite a speech: protecting the American people, no reprise of the Catastrophe, you can imagine the rest. Death to us monsters who would play God. I suspect he's going to be in trouble with his superiors for grandstanding. But he also said the tip came from someone 'inside one of these unlawful terrorist organizations' doing genetic engineering. I believed him."

"No," I said instantly. "It's just disinformation. Divide and conquer. They want us to think we have a mole who betrayed us."

"Or, " Kyle said, "we really do."

Susan called to us from an open upstairs window. I pretended not to hear her, saying quickly, "What have you found about the agent missing from the house? Anything else you can tell me?"

"No. Not yet. I—Susan! Stop yelling!"

It was a measure of Kyle's agitation that he shouted at his wife. Kyle never shouted.

Susan yelled back, "I asked if Caroline wants to come in for cake and coffee!"

"Yes," I shouted. "Thank you!"

Kyle stared at me. "I don't know any more than I've told you, Renata. Badgering me won't help."

I stared back. Badgering him, even if silently in Susan's presence, was all I had.

Kyle led me indoors. Susan served us strong coffee and delicious, homemade cake. But she wasn't herself, any more than Kyle was, although I would have bet my life that Kyle never told her anything about the Org.

"This is wonderful cake," I said to her.

"Thank you." A forced, too-bright smile.

Kyle stood abruptly. "I have a client arriving in a few minutes. Nice to see you, Caroline. Bye."

I didn't take the hint. Kyle stood there a few moments more and then left, looking displeased.

"Susan, could I have the recipe for this incredible cake?"

She blinked. "I didn't know you ever baked."

"I'm thinking of learning. Is this cake hard?"

"No. Yes, a little. I mean—I'll get the recipe for you." She stood.

I put my hand on hers, a first. "Susan—what's wrong? I don't mean to pry, but I couldn't help noticing how upset you and Kyle both seem . . . did I do something to offend you?"

It doesn't take much to get women like Susan, trusting and warm and open, to confide in you. An expression of concern, a touch of the hand, the promise of sympathy. She blurted out, "We might lose our house!"

"Your house?" Whatever I'd expected, it wasn't that.

She sat down again. "You're sweet to notice,

Caroline. But I've been diagnosed with . . . well, it doesn't matter what. I won't die. But the treatments Kyle wants me to have are new, the insurance doesn't cover them, and I won't use the girls' education funds. I won't. So we might have to sell the house, and even then . . . I don't know."

"I'm so sorry."

Susan put her hands over her face, but only for a moment before she rallied. She was stronger than I'd thought.

"It'll be all right. We'll manage. As long as we have each other, we'll be all right. And Caro, I'm so sorry to burden you with this. Don't worry about us."

Stronger, and good all the way through. She genuinely thought I'd find her confidence a worrisome burden because she would have if our situations were reversed. She genuinely thought I was a much nicer person than I was.

I said the meaningless thing people always say. "If I can do anything. . ."

"Thank you. Let me get that recipe for you. You'll love baking this cake."

In my apartment, I watched news streams all evening. Most were worthless: biased rehashings of the raid or anti-genemod rants full of wrong information. But Kyle was right about the grandstanding "first responder." Everything he said pointed to someone inside the Org tipping off DAS about the carrot station.

Who?

And how could I find out? I wasn't law enforcement, wasn't a lawyer, wasn't a scientist, wasn't even one of the anonymous rich donors funding the Org. I was just an amateur who believed in a cause. My role was to wait for whatever information the Org chose to give me about the raid.

Only . . . I couldn't. I had to know, had to put somewhere my anger over this latest outrage. Lisa Anderson, the carrot station, even Ian's death—they were all mixed up together in my mind, all cruelties that should not have happened. Not to self-sacrificing scientists and two children.

So . . . who?

Tom was an unknown quantity, at least to me. At our first lunch, he'd been insistent on talking to me about seafood, as if he knew something he shouldn't. He knew about the carrot station but not the other stations. Was it only coincidence that only the carrot station had been raided?

April was a ditz, brilliant on the computer and weird everywhere else. I remembered her saying as she told the long story about the time-as-a-bread-loaf lecture, "People *are* irrational." Was she? Enough to change her mind about the Org and betray us?

Jonas had been waiting a long time for a promotion within the Org. Did he think he'd waited too long, been passed over too often, most recently in favor of Kyle? Hadn't some American FBI agent turned mole for the Russians because he'd been passed over for promotion? I couldn't remember his name.

Kyle needed money or he would lose his house. But it couldn't be Kyle. No. It could not.

Or had leverage that I couldn't even imagine been brought to bear on those who'd worked at the carrot station? Louis Weinberg, Jean Cathcart, Miguel Gomez. The last two weren't even their real names. I knew nothing about Jean's or Miguel's personal lives, past lives, current beliefs. I had secrets, such as the information I got periodically from Joe Peck. Jean and Miguel and even Louis could have secrets, too.

If we didn't have a mole in our cell and the leak had come farther up the chain of command, then the feds could be negotiating with someone who could betray more of the Org. Or all of it. In that case, the carrot station had been just a preliminary raid.

I was a courier. Only that. I had no way to know anything, discover anything, do anything. All I could do was wait for instructions.

At 3:00 a.m. I bolted awake in my bedroom. I had just dreamed of giant carrots raping Lisa Anderson, a vision so poised between horror and triviality that it woke me in shame, in anger, in fear. My tee, panties, and sheets were soaked with sweat, the sheets twisted into grotesque shapes by my thrashing.

Who?

Jeremy phoned me early the next morning. "Renata, where are you?"

I didn't want to tell him that I was on my way to the Peninsula, driving blearily after three hours of sleep, careful to observe the speed limit. I wanted, pointlessly, to look at the newly lethal Blob. Maybe Joe would have additional information about its sudden deadliness. I said, "Why? Has something happened?"

"Yes, I think Naomi is going to call you any minute," he said, talking so fast that he sounded like a New Yorker, not a Montanan. "The tribal police arrested one of the men they think assaulted Lisa Anderson. Allegedly he was bragging in a bar, drunk on his ass. They're holding him but—"

"When? When did all this happen, and where?"

"Two a.m., at Randy's," he said, which was the

most significant part of the story. Randy's was a sleazy dive in Aberdeen, off tribal lands, and kidnapping is a federal crime. Tribal police could arrest the fucker but then needed U.S. law enforcement to take it from there.

Jeremy continued, "A U.S. deputy is holding him, but they need Lisa to ID him, and her mother won't let her look at so much as a photo to make an identification. The deputy's going to let the perp go. The deputy is a bigoted jackass. He says the arrest was illegal anyway—which it wasn't—and there'll be trouble for tribal police for making it."

"Christ!" I said. If the Quinault Nation would agree to cross-deputization of federal and tribal law enforcement, the tribal police would be on stronger ground. But I understood all the reasons why they didn't. Indigenous people don't have a lot of reason to share what power the state has allowed them.

Jeremy was still talking. "I'm sending Matt Carter out there to handle the legal end, but it'll be at least four hours 'til he arrives. Naomi will call to ask you to—"

"Phone's ringing now. I got it."

Naomi explained the situation. I told her I'd be there in twenty minutes. And to hell with the speed limit.

"No," Marina Anderson said. "No no *no*. Lisa's been through enough!"

Beyond the living room window of the Anderson house in Taholah, the ocean lay calm, choked with the Blob. Half of Taholah depended on salmon fishing for economic survival, and the Blob had made salmon runs puny this year. Marina and Naomi's living room had the stretched, thin feel of poverty looming in the corners. Naomi sat in a worn brown armchair, waiting for me to deal with Marina by using the one weapon I possessed and she did not.

Marina was not my favorite person on the reservation. I didn't mind her general rudeness to me, but she lacked her mother's clarity. Marina was swayed by the last person she'd talked to or the last thing she'd seen on TV. She had no self-control, and she made bad choices in men, in partying, in a petty-arrest record off the reservation. More than once, Jeremy had spent precious resources defending Marina. She loved Lisa but was not, in my view, an attentive mother. Naomi was, and now Naomi wanted me to use motherhood against Marina to change Marina's mind.

"No," Marina said again. "Not even a photo. Because it won't do any good! You should know that, white lady! White law never does any good for us!"

I didn't mention the good that Jeremy had done for her. This called for restraint, not one of my shining attributes. "I know, Marina. You're right about that. But in this case, I do know how you feel because—"

"Oh, right! You know how I feel because you have a daughter who was kidnapped and raped at thirteen years old!"

"No," I said. "I had a son who was killed right here at eleven years old."

It stopped her, as it was designed to. If she'd ever heard of Ian's death, she'd forgotten it, as she forgot everything not connected directly with herself. But she was silent for only a moment. "I don't believe you."

"It's true. He died here, a little farther down the beach. He was. . ."

I couldn't go on. I hated this, making Ian's death a tool to manipulate this grieving mother, *using* Ian. . .

"Tell me," Marina commanded, and the avidity in her voice made me want to hit her. To her, it was just a story, and a bad story happening to a Caucasian. But I saw the compassion in Naomi's eyes, and the need. Her sons had spent days looking for the rapists, and if they found the attackers before the law did, Naomi could lose her sons to violence or prison. I also thought of Lisa, in the room beyond. Was she awake? Listening?

"Tell me what happened to your son," Marina said again. And I did.

When I finished, Marina said, "So you're thinking I should be some kind of grateful because at least my kid is alive."

"No. I'm thinking that I would give anything to get justice for my kid, and I can't, and you can. Because we'll help you, fight for you, commit all the legal help we can, and if this fucker really did rape Lisa, he'll be locked up where he can't hurt any more children."

"You promise? You promise that if I let Lisa identify him, he'll go to prison?"

I said nothing. I knew, and she knew, that legal cases were never that simple.

"You promise?" Marina pushed. Was she looking for a "gotcha" moment? I couldn't give it to her.

"I promise we'll commit the resources, we'll follow through, we'll move heaven and earth to convict—*if* Lisa identifies this scumbag. Also, if Matt Carter—he's a U.S. attorney, he's good, and he's on his way here—can get this guy to flip, we might get all three of them."

"But you promise you'll do all that? You promise on Ian's grave?"

Naomi stood, finally showing her anger. I

didn't want that. I clenched my fist and said, "I promise on Ian's grave."

Only for you, Lisa.

"Still no," Marina said. "Too hard on Lisa. She isn't doing it."

She'd never intended to agree. And she'd made me relive the whole nightmare of Ian's death. A red mist took my brain, and I don't know what I would have done if the bedroom door hadn't opened. Lisa stood there, her face still bruised, one eye swollen and purpled. She wore a white nightgown with little flowers printed on it, but there was nothing childish about the look on her face. She was Naomi, sixty years ago.

"I am doing it," Lisa said. "Looking at pictures and then at live men. I'm doing it."

She paused; this was hard for her, but she was determined. Her bare toes below the hem of the nightgown curled in a tension that clutched at my heart.

"And Renata," she said in her girlish treble, "I'm sorry about your kid. That's really sad."

When I left, Matt Carter was talking gently to Lisa, who pressed close to her grandmother's side. I didn't stay for the mug-shot identification that, eventually, would be followed by a lineup

ID in person. I felt as exhausted as if I'd run a marathon.

I drove to the beach and stood on the low bluff overlooking the Pacific. Joe wasn't there. The tide was in and floating logs drifted aimlessly on the stony shore. The Blob floated serenely on the sea.

I stood there until my eyes burned from light reflected off the water. But whatever I was looking for was not here. There was nothing left of Ian here, where he'd died. What I had left of him was in my work for the Org.

"It's not right. *Those people—they can't grow enough food. I can sell a lot of my stuff and donate the money!*"

I got in my car and drove home.

2032: SEATTLE, WASHINGTON

JEAN CATHCART and Miguel Gomez were charged with "bioterrorism." They pled guilty. The judge, who seemed saner than most, recognized that although creating GMO carrots was classed as terrorism, neither Jean nor Miguel was likely to release weaponized pathogens or open fire in a crowded mall. He released them on bail, which was paid, ostensibly, by their families.

"They're finished with the Org," April said, stating the obvious. "Everybody will recognize them now."

No one answered her. This was the first meeting of the cell since the raid. In the late afternoon, April, Jonas, Tom, and I sat at a table in the "chess club," waiting for Kyle. It wasn't like him to be late, and all of us felt uneasy.

Did the others have the same thoughts I did: Was it *you* who betrayed the station to DAS? You,

Tom, as a planted informant? You, Jonas, from being passed over for promotion? You, April, from some ditzy theory? Or was it Kyle, absent now and in bad financial difficulty?

Minutes snailed by.

Tom asked, "Anybody want to play chess?"

April said, "I'll play if you show me how the pieces move."

Tom didn't even answer that.

April said, "Ooo-kay. Jonas, why didn't they arraign Louis with Jean and Miguel?"

"My guess is they're retaining him as a material witness. Indefinitely."

We considered that nasty piece of legal imprisonment without trial, and we all shut up.

When Kyle finally arrived, he looked as if he hadn't slept in days. His clothes had the rumpled look of having just gotten off a plane or train, and I wondered where, and with whom, he'd been conferring.

"The teff and wheatgrass stations are safe," he said, without preliminaries. "The Org has no idea how DAS got information about the carrot station. Neither do I."

Silence. I broke it, finally. "Are you thinking it was one of us?"

"No. I'm not. I know you all."

Shrewd and informed judgement or wishful trust? I no longer knew.

Kyle continued, "I think it must have come from farther up the line."

Tom said, "Then why doesn't DAS have enough information to raid a bunch of stations?"

"I don't know. But we're going to carry on. April, report."

She looked surprised at his brusque tone and then did her usual thing of morphing from ditzy April to tech-savvy April. It always startled me. "Posts from all sides have ramped up, information and disinformation both, but no shifts in tone. The sane anti-GMO groups say the carrot station is only the tip of the iceberg, that there are more attempts to create dangerous crops by people who are at best deluded, at worst tools of agribusiness trying to rise from ashes. A lot of worry about cross-pollination and genetic drift. I'm counting Greenpeace among my saner chickens. The—*what*, Caroline?"

"Nothing," I said. Icebergs with ashes and chickens. Well, the Org didn't use April because she had a firm grasp of metaphor.

April scowled at me. "The lunatic ecoterrorists say that the carrot station was either the work of Americans who hate the United States and want to destroy it, or foreign powers that hate the United States and want to destroy it, or signs of the End Times before Armageddon, or the first stream in a river of poison that will drown us all, or . . . you get the idea. There are also a lot of posts that I think are coming from overseas, subtle clues in the coding, that seem aimed at getting people to take down the federal government for not protecting us enough. DAS has put out only the bland statements you saw on TV. Nobody has anything out there about the details of the carrots' engineering, although a lot of sites have invented stuff. The carrots produce arsenic, or cyanide, or—this one made me laugh out loud—hemlock. Hemlock isn't even in the same biological family as—"

Kyle interrupted her. "What have we put out?"

"What you and I crafted. Pro-GMO, some with actual statistics and some with developing-world heartbreak stories. I used that quote you gave me from Norman Borlaug about environmental lobbyists of the western nations being elitists who have never experienced genuine hunger. The posts aren't too virulent, nothing that would attract attention compared to others, but I multiplied them by three times the usual rate. I also got our sympathizers in Kenya and India to put up fresh pictures. Don't worry, Kyle, I covered my tracks. Nobody can trace the requests to me."

"Good. I may want you to move the computer soon."

Only Kyle knew where April's computer was located, how its encryption worked, or what security precautions surrounded approaching it. My private theory was that unless the building was opened with a special D, it would blow up, but maybe this was just imagination. Or too much TV.

"Move it?" April asked. "To where?"

Kyle didn't answer, of course, and April began fiddling with a chess piece, trying to get it to stand on its head, her pretty young face scowling—should our safety rest with someone so young and so cavalier about using the undernets? Tom watched her intently. From romantic interest? Or federal interest? And when had I become so paranoid?

Jake's voice in my head: *"You've always been paranoid, Renata."*

When the meeting finished, Kyle said, "Stay a minute, Caroline."

The others all stopped moving and looked at me. Then, obedient, they left, chatting innocuously about chess matches that had not occurred, dispersing to their regular lives.

Kyle closed the door. "Have you been contacted by the press? Do we need to work around that?"

"The press? Why?"

Kyle's weary face looked briefly surprised. "Jake. Wait—you don't know?"

"Know what?" Suddenly my heart hit painfully against my chest wall.

"The accident. You *don't* know. Jake was in a skiing accident. He—"

"Jake doesn't ski!"

"Apparently not. He slammed into a tree. He'll be all right, but he broke both legs in multiple places and punctured his spleen. The press is going wild because that new movie was supposed to start shooting tomorrow and there's no way he can do it, which is going to cost everybody large amounts of money. Don't look like that, Renata, the report I saw said he'll be all right. But if the press is seeking you out for some stupid 'fresh angle'—"

"Nobody has contacted me," I said. What had my face looked like?

"Okay. Look, skip the next few meetings, just in case. I'll have Jonas cover your stations for now."

I nodded, keeping my face rigid. Jake badly hurt . . .

Kyle removing me from my stations . . .

Jake badly hurt . . .

I drove home. A reporter lurked by the door of my apartment building, camdrone and recorder at the ready. She looked like a big cat with an outlier sheep. I said, "No comment," and went upstairs to call Jake. No answer. I tried Dylan, but he didn't answer, either. I couldn't wait for Dylan to get back to me; I had to know the truth about Jake's condition. I made another call.

"Portland Police, East Precinct."

"May I please speak to Dylan Sanderson?"

Silence. Then the voice said stiffly, "Who is calling, please?"

"May I speak to Dylan Sanderson?"

"Dylan Sanderson is no longer on the force. Who is—"

I clicked off. They could trace the call, of course, but I didn't know why they would. I didn't know anything else, either. When and why had Dylan left the force? His cell went again to voice-mail. I left another message.

Online celebrity-news sites said so many conflicting things about Jake's accident, mixed with so much speculation, that they were worthless. I did, however, learn which hospital he was in. I booked a 6:30 a.m. flight to Los Angeles for the next day. Then I went online and searched for Dylan's name. A Portland newspaper had a small story, dated a month ago.

THIRD OFFICER CHARGED IN "DIRTY COP RING" SCANDAL

A third officer, Dylan Sanderson, has been charged with larceny, extortion, and evidence tampering in the ongoing scandal at Portland's East Precinct. Sanderson, who is the brother of movie star Jake Sanderson, was arrested last night at his home. Arraignment is set for tomorrow. Sanderson, like the other two accused officers, allegedly stole street drugs worth thousands of dollars from a police evidence room, sold them undercover to known dealers, and pocketed the money. There is speculation that Sanderson may strike a plea deal in which he names other police officers involved. "We don't know how high this goes," said Commissioner Jane Rivera, "but I can assure the public that all—"

Was Dylan still in jail? Out on bail? Repeated phone calls, for most of the night, failed to reach either him or Jake. The hospital, undoubtedly besieged, would tell me nothing.

I wasn't even sure why I so desperately needed to see Jake, to be sure he was all right. We'd been divorced for years. We no longer had Ian as a tie between us. I wasn't even sure whether he was living with whoever had replaced the women who'd replaced Sage Scott. But the image of him lying helpless with two broken legs, or in major surgery for his spleen, unable to do the work that gave his life meaning the way that the Org gave meaning to mine—at that image, a primitive and urgent need to see him seized me like a boa constrictor.

People aren't rational, April said so often that we were sick of hearing it. Irrational online, irrational offline, irrational in my painful heart.

A few hours of bad sleep before I made a cup of strong coffee and packed. As I drove to the airport, my dashboard news interrupted the weather report with a breaking story. A terrorist, a Ukrainian extremist in pursuit of some insane vision or other, had opened fire at SeaTac airport and killed five passengers and two desk agents at the Southwest check-in before being taken down by an off-duty cop dropping off his wife for a flight to Kansas City. The airport was being evacuated and shut down until further notice.

I pulled over and rebooked from Portland, just in case. The first flight I could get didn't leave until midnight. I took it, even though the only seats left were in first class. I don't fly first class. Why were so many people flying from Portland to L.A. in the middle of the night? *Stay home, all of you. Stay home.*

Seattle at dawn is eerily beautiful. Not many delivery or cab drones were flying yet. The rising sun put a glow on Elliott Bay, gradual and mysterious, as if the waters were being created that moment. The skyscrapers, wrapped in light mist, seemed like enchanted towers. It never lasted long. Eventually, an ordinary city emerged that, like all American cities, was still fighting to regain itself after the Catastrophe. Seattle, high tech rather than agribusiness, was hit less than most, but a lot of civic upkeep still got neglected. The sun rose, and I drove to a potholed parking lot in a mostly empty strip mall. The parking lot was half full of a tent city of people made homeless by automation. A lone cop bot silently patrolled the rows of tents.

One of my Org cell phones sat in its lockbox at a Keep It Safe! It contained no new messages from Kyle, but the lockbox also held something completely unprecedented: a small padded envelope, addressed to Caroline Denton. The upper-left corner of the envelope was smeared with Tiffany Teal paint.

This was not how we communicated.

I sat in my car, holding the envelope for a long time before deciding this wasn't how DAS communicated, either. And if DAS knew enough about us to get an envelope into an Org lockbox, I was already toast. Or, if the envelope came from some ecoterrorist group that had infiltrated us, and whatever was inside would kill me, they knew who I was and could do that any time they chose. I got out of my car, took a deep breath, pulled my shirt over my mouth and nose, and opened the envelope.

Inside was the toothbrush I had taken from the lost house, along with two folded sheets of paper, each densely covered with Ts, Cs, As, Gs. The papers were headed SUBJECT 1, SUBJECT 2. Both were DNA code from the Standard DNA Identification Genomic Section, a manageable, distinctive stretch of the long human genome routinely used to identify individuals. Jean Cathcart—now out on bail under her real name and so never "Jean Cathcart" again—must have done the sequencing and sent this to me just before the raid on the carrot station. Two IDs—did that mean that two different people had used the same toothbrush? Ugh.

I looked again at the papers. On the bottom of each was a notation: SALIVA 99% and HANDLE 53%. Confidence levels regarding the accuracy of the sequences. I looked again at the sheet labeled HANDLE. The DNA ID, as far as I could remember, was mine.

Duh. I had picked up the toothbrush to put it in my pocket. My hand had been sweaty. Probably the toothbrush owner's DNA was on the handle, too, confused with mine. But the saliva ID would be the toothbrush user's alone.

It might or might not be in the National Data Bank of DNA that had been slowly compiled over the last twelve years. Some people, including very vocal members of Congress, had fought bitterly to keep the NDBDNA from existing at all. Invasion of privacy, dangerous precedent, etc. Law enforcement, which had its own congressional champions, had won that one, aided by part of a very divided AMA. People whose DNA was on file with the NDBDNA fell into several classes: cops, firefighters, military, criminals, sex offenders, people who taught or worked with children, and—voluntarily—everyone who chose to enroll themselves or their child so that a body could be identified if it was murdered, burned in a house fire, or abducted by aliens and returned as a zombie.

The Org did not turn down members just because they were on file in the NDBDNA. If DAS caught us, our constructed identities were too flimsy anyway. The fake ID, cell phone, and credit card I had for "Caroline Denton" could satisfy a casual traffic stop or drug arrest, but not a genuine investigation. The Org didn't have the resources for that.

So, the DNA from the wandering house might or might not be on file. If it was, I needed someone authorized to use the NDBDNA. I knew someone who would: Joe Peck's uncle-in-law, Gray Carter. Gray, a white cop, was married to Joe's aunt, a registered tribal member. They lived off the reservation in Bellingham, north of Seattle. Jeremy had once defended Gray's sister in court, and Gray occasionally ran IDs for us, under the table.

He would think this request came from Jeremy, and I wouldn't tell him different.

But Bellingham would have to wait. I put the papers in my pocket and drove south to SeaTac, to wait at a nearby Starbucks until they reopened the airport. If I were among the first ones in, maybe I could wheedle a harried desk clerk into putting me on a flight to L.A. earlier than the one I'd booked from Portland.

It didn't work. In mid-afternoon I gave up and drove to Portland, arriving just after sunset. I rented a car and drove to Dylan's building.

From the outside, I could see lights in his apartment. But when I identified myself to the smart building, it said pleasantly, "I'm sorry, access is denied."

"By whom?"

"I'm sorry, access is denied."

You can't argue with a building. Nor with a person who refuses to admit you exist. My face had been erased from the building's recognition file, which only could have been done by Dylan himself. When I tried to slip in behind a resident, the building let out a blatting alarm and shrieked, "Access denied! Access denied!" I was stopped in the lobby by a roboguard. "If you do not immediately exit the building, I will restrain you and summon the police." I immediately exited the building.

Dylan did not answer his cell. If I could have, I would have thrown gravel at his window, but he lived on the fifth floor, and the building told me that if I did not move twenty feet away from its walls, it was going to summon the police.

I left, puzzled and hurt. Why was Dylan doing this? I knew he was home; every window in his apartment blazed with light. Was he so ashamed of having been kicked off the force as a dirty cop that he couldn't face me? Was Jake far more injured than I knew, maybe dying, and Dylan was afraid to tell me? Or was Dylan even now by Jake's bedside and someone else was housesitting his apartment? But that didn't explain my being erased from his building's access list.

All the awkward dinners I'd shared with Dylan had been prompted by an unpleasant emotion: guilt that I didn't really like Jake's little brother, even as I exploited him to glean scraps of information about my ex-husband. Did Dylan realize that and finally let resentment about it boil over?

No answers. An online search turned up no further news stories about dirty cops in the East Precinct. The internet war over the carrot station still raged, and I saw at least two pieces that were probably April's. I also found a story about Lisa

Anderson: RAPIST OF NATIVE AMERICAN GIRL PLEADS GUILTY. So that scumbag had been identified, had made a plea bargain, and—I hoped—had flipped. Jeremy would keep pressure on the cops to find the other two men.

I drove to the airport, fell asleep sitting up in a highly uncomfortable chair, and eventually boarded my flight to L.A., landing at 2:30 in the morning. I splurged on an auto-helio cab to the hospital.

"I'd like to go upstairs to see a patient—"

"No visitors except spouses until 8:00 a.m. Are you the spouse?"

"No, I'm—"

"No visitors except spouses until 8:00 a.m."

She was an elderly ogre with pink hair, old-fashioned glasses, and the general mien of a prison guard. I smiled as disarmingly as I could. "Look, I just arrived from the airport and it's imperative that I see Jake Sanderson. I'm—"

"No visitors except spouses until 8:00 a.m., and after that no one is allowed to see Jake Sanderson except those on the list. Are you on the list?"

I thought as rapidly as exhaustion permitted. "Yes. I'm his agent, Morgan Tarryn."

The dragon possessed an unfortunate knowledge of the movie industry. "You're not Morgan Tarryn. He's a man."

So much for gender-neutral names. "I meant

that I'm with the Morgan Tarryn Agency. He sent me with some important papers for Jake to sign as soon as—"

"Security! Security!"

A bored lobby guard sprang to life, followed by a more formidable security bot than the one in Dylan's building. This one looked like it could handle a Ranger platoon. The human guard said, "What's the trouble?"

"She's trying to fake her way into seeing a patient, and she's not on his list!"

The guard squinted at me. The bot was running its tentacles all around my body without actually touching me. Its lights all flashed green. I had no weapons, explosives, or controlled substances. The guard said, "Well, if she's not on the list, she can't go up."

"That's what I told her!" the gorgon said triumphantly. "Now, you, leave the building!"

"She can stay in the lobby," the guard said. They locked eyes, and I suddenly realized this was a turf war, possibly of long standing. The guard shook his head and said to me scornfully, "Volunteers."

Cerberus began to sputter at him, and I retreated to a lobby chair to think what I could do next. Awake for most of the last twenty-four hours, I didn't even realize when I slipped into cramped and twitchy sleep.

Daylight flooded the hospital lobby, people bustled through, and Morgan Tarryn stood disbelievingly in front of me. "Renata?"

"Hello, Morgan. I came to—"

A good agent is perceptive. "Of course you did. Come on, I'll take you up."

The harpy behind the desk shrieked, "Mr. Tarryn, she's not on the list!"

"She is now."

Trolls, guards, nurses, even cleaning bots parted before Morgan Tarryn like waves in the Red Sea. In the elevator I said, "How is he?"

"Okay. Not more than that. The surgery on his spleen was successful, but he'll need a lot of physical therapy to walk again. And we lost the picture."

I didn't care about the picture. "But he will walk again?"

"If he works at it. Probably. We're waiting for the results of some tests."

"God, Morgan—"

"I didn't know you two still saw each other."

His tone alerted me. "Who is she? Is she there now?"

"No. You'd know if she was there now. Gina Jones."

I blinked. Gina Jones was huge, a first-magnitude star, preternaturally beautiful, fifteen years younger than Jake. Or me. All at once I was aware of my ancient jeans, baggy sweater, graying hair.

A uniformed guard stood outside the door to Jake's room, but no reporters—not on the list. My first sight of Jake wasn't good. One leg was up in traction; did that mean he'd injured his spine? His face, never classically handsome, was swollen, bruised, and unshaven, his hair dirty. He looked like a drunk who'd just lost a serious fight.

But his eyes widened when he saw me, and a light came into them.

"Renata. What are you doing here?"

"What are you doing skiing into trees? How stupid is that?"

"Really stupid. Hey, Morgan."

Morgan waved some papers at him. "I just need a minute, Jake, but first I need the bathroom." He left.

"The very spirit of tact," Jake said. "Why are you—"

"I don't know. To see just how stupid you actually were. To see that you're okay, which you don't look like you are."

"It looks worse than it is. My spine is all right. I got the news last night. I'll walk again, after some physical therapy."

I could resume breathing, but it took a moment.

Jake said softly, "Hey. It's good of you to come."

Our eyes held each other. The moment spun out, both eternal and too short, until I deliberately broke it. "Jake, I stopped in Portland. Dylan won't see me. Why not?"

Jake turned his head to look at the ceiling. "My fault."

"Yours?"

"I didn't handle Dylan well. I gave him hell for getting involved in that evidence theft and blowing his career. He gave me hell for being 'high and mighty' about being a success when he's a failure. It was pretty bad. You're just collateral damage."

Just collateral damage. And I'd made the trip to Portland because I was concerned about Dylan. Anger rose in me, but Jake looked so miserable that I pushed it down and said quietly, "Dylan's always been jealous of you."

"I know."

"Not your fault, Jake."

"So say you."

He turned his head and there it was again, that look in his eyes, that look between us. Something moved in my chest. But before I could say anything, there was a commotion in the hall.

Not Morgan returning. A big commotion.

Gina Jones swept into the room with an entourage: bodyguard, publicist, astrologer, sorcerer's apprentice, or whoever these people were. At 9:00 in the morning, she was in full makeup and a slinky dress, eyeball-kick beautiful. Perfume assaulted my nostrils, musk and gardenia. "Jake! My God, you look awful!"

"Thanks," Jake said dryly. The bodyguard was staring at me, assessing. I slipped toward the door.

Jake didn't say anything to stop me, for which I was grateful.

Always good to recognize a lost cause.

2032: SEATTLE, WASHINGTON

GRAY CARTER phoned to say he would meet me at his sister-in-law's house on the reservation, where he and his wife were visiting her family. He gave me careful directions. I had no work reason to drive to the Quinault Nation from Seattle, so I told Jeremy that I didn't feel well and was going home for the rest of the day.

"You don't look well," he said, which was convenient but unflattering. It was also true. I looked like hell, and compared to the fresh memory of Gina Jones as she bent to kiss Jake, it was a very low circle of hell.

"Probably just a cold coming on," I said. "I'll be back tomorrow."

"Get some rest, drink fluids."

The weather had turned cold, although October cold in Seattle meant something different than the cold I had grown up with back East. Still, frost made lacy patterns on the windshield of my car, and the Olympic Peninsula would be very wet. I dug out boots and a pea coat from the back of my disorderly closet. From a Keep It Safe! along the way, I opened a lockbox that was not one of the Org's. However that padded mailer with the toothbrush had gotten into my Org lockbox, its appearance was a deviation from routine. If there had been one deviation, there could be others. I wanted to be prepared. The items from my lockbox fit into my boot.

By the time I reached the reservation, dark clouds obscured the setting sun. Julie's family didn't live in Taholah, but in an isolated cabin. I drove along narrow, unpaved back roads with trees crowding either side and meeting overhead. A tall, unsmiling man met me outside the cabin, and I had the impression he wasn't pleased to have me there. He insisted on seeing ID before he led me inside. The living room/kitchen had a much more rustic look than Naomi's house, and some of the furniture looked homemade. Gray sprawled in a chair, reading.

"Hey, Renata," he said, rising. "Julie and them have gone visiting. Thanks, Dave."

Dave left, still unsmiling. Gray shrugged. "That's Dave. Never was thrilled with me marrying into the family."

It didn't seem to bother him. Gray had the perfect temperament for a good cop: not excitable, not prone to taking things personally, accepting that the world was not the way he'd like it to be but nonetheless acting as fairly as he could. It was also the perfect temperament for a white man who'd married a member of a Native tribe.

"It's good to see you, Gray."

"You, too. But I hope you won't be offended if I cut this short. I told Julie I'd go on up to her mother's after I gave you this." He pulled an index card from his pocket and handed it to me. It had a name that I didn't recognize and hadn't expected to: James Allen McKay.

"I ran him at the station," Gray said. "No priors, no outstanding warrants, a home address in Olympia. There, I wrote it on the bottom of the card. What's this about, Renata? Why is Jeremy interested in him? He attack an Indian girl?"

Married six years to Julie, yet Gray still hadn't learned to say, "Native American" or "tribal." I began to see why Julie's family "wasn't thrilled." Yet I knew the marriage was happy.

April, in my head: *People aren't rational.*

"No, no attack that I know of. Jeremy asked me to get this identity off the DNA but under the table, and he didn't tell me why. I promise your name will never come up."

Gray never took his eyes off me. "I believe you.

147

But you know you can't use that in court, or anything it leads to. Fruit of the poisoned tree."

"I know. Jeremy knows."

"Well, I trust you," Gray said, and I saw the moment he put the whole thing out of his mind. A talent I often envied, although it also explained why Gray would never make detective.

In my car, I tried my cell. No coverage. I would have to get closer to Taholah, or back toward Seattle. Impatient, I drove toward the more populated coast.

Waves lapped at the ocean, but no whitecaps. Water and sky were steel gray, smelling of rain. At a deserted bluff a mile from the village, I got Wi-Fi, entered the tribal password, and Googled James Allen McKay. There wasn't much, but he was named in a family photo with a laughing woman and a little boy.

I zoomed in on the picture, squinted at it, tried to make it go away. All at once, the car felt like an iceberg, and I was adrift on it. I *recognized* James Allen McKay. Floppy hair like pop star Canton Sparks, nose too big to look like Canton Sparks, thin lips, and blue eyes. He was the "cop" in the dark suit who, accompanied by a uniformed officer, had questioned me in the wandering house in Pioneer Square.

James Allen McKay had used the toothbrush I'd taken from the house. But if he was an Org agent, why would he be outside the house, with another cop?

No. *No.*

I dug further online. I'm not April, but there are tricks you learn to get information that supposedly has been deleted. James Allen McKay worked for the Department of Agriculture Security. For DAS.

The lost house had been bait. DAS knew—must have known—that eventually someone from the Org would recognize the Tiffany Teal paint on the windowsill. That someone would have the means to enter the locked house, in order to check on whatever agent should be inside. Then all DAS had to do was follow that person, for days or weeks, to see where they went. And I had led them to the carrot station, the teff station, Kyle's house, the ersatz chess club where our cell met.

I was the mole, the leaker, the betrayer. Me.

I pounded my fists on the steering wheel until they screamed with pain.

No—I had to pull myself together. Think what to do next. Had DAS agents followed me onto tribal lands? Did they know about Joe? Maybe not; Joe had a legitimate job with NOAA that justified his taking samples of algae and ocean water. And it wasn't that easy to follow someone on tribal lands.

But—NOAA had had its funding cut, and yet

Joe went on sampling. What did DAS make of that? Had I betrayed not only my cell and the scientists at two stations but also Joe Peck?

I had to warn him. I couldn't call Kyle because I didn't have a Caroline Denton phone with me, but I was here, at the Quinault Nation, and I could warn Joe in person. That was a thing I could do. Now.

He wasn't on the beach. I didn't even know where he lived. I drove to Naomi's.

"Renata. Why are—" Naomi stopped and looked at me. She took my arm, pulled me in her front door, and closed it. "Tell me."

I shook my head, unable for a moment to speak. Then I got out, "Joe."

Her fingers tightened on my arm. "Joe? Is he dead?"

"No, no. I . . . I need to see him. Now."

She didn't ask why. Her sunken eyes searched my face, and then she said, "Wait here. Sit."

I did, and she left. Fifteen minutes later, the longest fifteen minutes of my life, she was back with Joe.

"Tell me," he said, echoing Naomi. He listened with what seemed to me preternatural calm. Didn't he realize . . .

He did.

"All right," he said. "They made you. We go now. It's sooner than we planned, but we're ready."

"Go . . . go where? What's ready?"

"Please get her a warmer coat. Really warm. Her boots are okay."

Naomi didn't even ask why. She brought a hooded parka and wool scarf.

"Joe, what is . . . I don't understand."

"You will. Put those on."

I obeyed. I didn't see any other good options.

"This way," Joe said, and led me through the tiny kitchen out the back door.

It had started to rain. I thought, *The Blob will break up now*, and wondered that I could, even for a moment, think of anything other than the mess I'd created.

I stopped under a grove of trees and said, "I'm not going any farther until you tell me where I'm headed."

In the rainy dusk, I couldn't see Joe's face as he turned toward me. But I heard his voice. "Org regional headquarters."

"What?" I couldn't have heard him right. The rain, the ocean waves on the beach, the hood of my parka . . .

"We're going to Org regional HQ. I know you thought I was just an Org grunt, like you. I'm not. Come on, Renata. Move."

"But where . . . how . . ."

"Headquarters is on tribal land. Can you think of a better place to hide something?"

"But you don't . . . the tribes don't . . ."

"Yes, we do. *I* do—I'm a scientist. Many tribal members don't like GMOs, but they know that GMOs are the only thing that might save the land and ocean from the agribusinesses that destroyed them once."

The enemy of my enemy is my friend.

I had always prided myself on my "good instincts" about people. Now I saw that I had none. I had misjudged Joe, had misjudged the Quinault Nation, had misjudged pretty much everyone. And that, I further realized, included Dylan Sanderson.

Because DAS hadn't just sent a drivie house to wander aimlessly around Seattle in the hopes that it would encounter a random Org member before city police were called to stop it. That "lost" house had been sent straight to me. That was why it had Tiffany Teal paint on the windowsill. Dylan had committed evidence theft and pleaded guilty, yet he was not in jail. He'd cut a deal. To cut a deal with a district attorney, you had to have something to offer, maybe something more than just the names of two other dirty cops. Dylan had offered me.

"Come on," Joe said again, and I followed him through the dark rain, out of Taholah and into the woods.

———————

"Regional headquarters" was nothing like I had imagined. No large gleaming lab, no army of scientists, no twenty-four-hour armed security. All that must exist elsewhere. And I didn't know how many regions the Org had, or how much territory each covered.

We had slogged through what seemed miles of dripping trees, tripping over brush. If there was a trail, I didn't see it in the thick dark. But Joe moved confidently, sure of where he was going, pulling me along by my rain-slicked hand.

Headquarters was a wooden cabin, little more than a shack, in deep woods. No road that I could see.

"*This?* Joe—"

He ignored me and fished a D from his pocket. It pinged softly as it unlocked the door. Lights went on inside, and I could see that the D in his hand looked nothing like mine. Not just any Org member could get in here.

The inside, including the door, was a concrete bunker with a steel door. A Quinault woman in jeans and heavy wool sweater rose from the only chair, which faced a computer with a coffee machine beside it. One corner held a bed, small refrigerator, reading lamp. Nothing else.

She said, "Joe?" And then, "Oh, gods—now?"

"Yes. I've been compromised."

"*You?* Who else?"

"I don't know. But if they've found me, they've found most of—"

"I know." She stared at me hard. "Who's this? Was she the breach?"

"Not her fault. Catherine, we have to launch now."

"How much?"

Joe hesitated; his face said this was a critical, irreversible decision that had to be made. "All of it."

"Okay." She sat at the computer and began to key. Two more screens lit up. The computer said in a mechanical voice, "Satellite contact."

"Joe," I said, because it was impossible to stay silent, "if you contact a satellite, won't DAS be able to—"

"Yes," he said. And then, "Wait."

The computer said, "Missiles armed."

Missiles? My breath tangled in my throat and would not come out.

Joe took pity on me. "Not warheads."

Catherine gave a short, bitter laugh.

More commands, more typing, and she rose. "Done. Let's go."

Nothing seemed to have happened. I stood, ignorant as grass, and as helpless. Catherine shrugged into a jacket and picked up a paperback book: *The Gulag Archipelago*. She put it in her pocket, opened the door, and, without a word to either of us, melted into the woods.

I followed Joe outside and away from the cabin. "You didn't lock the door."

"Doesn't matter. Come on. They'll be here soon."

He meant DAS. I said, "So they did follow me? By drone?"

"Probably. But either way, they'll come here soon. Get behind that tree."

It was a huge sycamore, a few leaves still on the branches and writhing in the rain. I moved partly behind it, watching Joe.

He did something, and an explosion rocked the ground, the tree, me. The sky lit up and smoke rose from the direction the cabin had stood. A second later, we were in darkness again, a wet blackness more complete than I had ever known.

"Joe," I said into that blackness, "please tell me what's going on!"

"Soon," he said, a disembodied voice. "Right now, we have to move."

Everything on me ached from our previous trek; I was not Joe's age. His hand grasped mine—I didn't know how he even found it in the darkness—and again he pulled me along. I kept tripping, but at least the rain had stopped.

After fifteen or twenty or thirty minutes, I heard water. Joe turned on a flashlight, sweeping the low beam over the ground. We were beside the Quinault River—or maybe it was the Queets or the Raft; by now I had absolutely no sense of direction. Joe drew a flat-bottomed rowboat from under brush and helped me into it. He turned off the flashlight. In the dark we half drifted, half rowed down the river.

I sat shivering in the prow, knowing that I must not talk. Sound carried over water. The watery silence felt apocalyptic, as if the world had ended and all that was left was this boat, darkness, and the river.

Eternity passed. Slowly.

Lights on the shore, from a collection of houses, but not enough houses to be Taholah or Queets. So this *was* the Raft River. Nothing stirred on the riverbanks. Ahead, ocean waves lapped softly.

Joe paddled more vigorously now. The tide was going out, which helped. He seemed to know exactly where he was going. I pushed out of my mind visions of a riptide taking us, or a suicide/murder to ensure silence, or simple death by hypothermia.

Joe's breathing became more labored. He was working hard. I heard another sound: a helicopter.

Joe said softly, his first words in an hour, "The chopper's over land. Don't worry."

Don't worry? *Don't worry?* I was at sea in a small rowboat at night, a fugitive from federal justice, and I shouldn't worry?

Once, long ago during a fight with Jake, he

told me that I was "too intense." I'd said that it was impossible to be too intense about a just cause that you believed in. Jake retorted that no, it wasn't impossible, because intensity can cloud judgment. The fight had gone on from there, until we were both exhausted.

Feeling Joe strain at the oars, I knew that I hadn't known what intensity really was.

A light, somewhere ahead. A boat. Joe pulled toward it, and then someone was hauling me, frozen and numb, over the side of a fishing boat. I collapsed onto the deck. Someone yanked me, not gently, upright and pushed me into a cabin. At first, all I knew was that it was blessedly warm.

Someone handed me a cup of hot coffee. Someone else said, "God, Joe—who the fuck is she?" I didn't hear his answer.

The boat was moving.

"If we're boarded, she'll have to go in the hole."

Then a woman's voice. "Let her be for now."

I drained the coffee, even though my stiff fingers could barely hold the cup and even though I didn't take it black. The liquid burn in my throat was welcome. "No," I said, "don't let me be. I want answers. Joe?"

"Okay," he said.

The "missiles" were weapons of war, but not the war anyone expected. They'd been launched from four different locations, by a signal sent through a communications satellite, using software that Org hackers had piggybacked onto the satellite's software. I hadn't known we had hackers that good.

The missiles were self-exploding cannisters that scattered a genetically altered virus over the ocean. For billions of years, viruses have evolved to make war on bacteria, and vice versa. This particular virus was engineered to infect *Pseudonitzschia* and change the diatom so that it could not make use of the bacteria that caused it to make domoic acid. The bloom would remain, but it would not produce toxin.

"That's the GMO least likely to be detected by DAS," Joe finished. "And the one I've worked on."

"All these years, you were—"

"Yes. Renata, please don't—"

"I'm not crying. I'm not going to cry."

Joe studied the dark water, looking away from the scene I was not going to make. Jake was the only man I've ever known who could meet an emotional scene head on. And some feelings are too deep for theatrics.

I said quietly, "No more toxicity in blooms. If—"

If this had happened a decade ago, Ian might not have died.

"Yes, if all goes well. We built the GMO with a gene drive to spread the allele quicker and more reliably. But, Renata, we planned this escape as a last resort, and we didn't plan for you. We can't—"

"You don't have to," I said. "I planned, too."

2032: VICTORIA, CANADA

IN THE MORNING, I sat in the boat's tiny cabin, eating a bagel and cream cheese that did not taste like the ones in New York. They never do. *Stay below decks*, the woman called "Jenny" had told me, *in case of drone or satellite surveillance. This is a fishing boat, and you're no Quinault fisher.*

Joe slipped onto the bench across from me. "Let me see them."

I pushed across the table the Canadian passport and Barclay bank card in the name of Ellen Mary Tompkins. Both had my picture, thumbprint, retinal scan. They were slightly damp from the time in my boot.

"And nobody in the Org knows about this identity. You got these on your own."

"Yes. Jeremy Hardwick doesn't know about them, either."

"Facial recognition at Passport Control will flag you as Renata Black."

"Canada refuses to share facial-recog data with the United States. They don't like our policies on immigration. And I've never been in Canada before. I won't be in the data bank."

"Renata, if—"

"No. I've endangered you enough already, Joe. And I can't go home." I paused. "Can you?"

"Depends. If DAS hasn't learned my identity—"

"I've thought about that. I never told Dylan about you. He's the one who first put me in touch with the Org years ago, but I never told him anything about it, or you."

He nodded, his face blank. The closeness, the sense of a shared plight that I'd felt from him last night, had evaporated. I might have been a thousand yards away.

"If that's true, Renata—" and he must have known how his doubt stung "—then maybe eventually I can go home. If not, there are tribes in Canada that will accept me. But not you."

"I know. Just set me ashore in the harbor. And Joe—will you do one more thing for me? Get word to Jake Sanderson that I'm alive and safe?"

Joe looked at me for longer than was comfortable. I couldn't read his expression, but it seemed that he saw more than I wanted. Finally he said, "Okay."

The boat chugged on up the Strait of Juan de Fuca toward Victoria, Canada.

At the government building at Victoria harbor, I got in the line labeled RETURNING CITIZENS.

"Name?"

"Ellen Mary Tompkins."

The inspector flipped through, looking for the exit stamp. It was there, dated a week ago. That much the fishing boat had been able to do for me. That and a small, nearly empty suitcase, because travelers carried luggage.

"Purpose of your trip to the United States?"

"To visit relatives."

He glanced at me, flicked his eyes at the photo, and stamped the passport. He said, "Welcome home, Ms. Tompkins," and I was a Canadian citizen.

I took a drivie to a cheaper hotel in a cheaper section of town than the touristy harbor, and checked in. All day I watched news, switching channels promiscuously, hoping to find something about DAS' war on the Org.

Nothing.

I had no internet access, or I might have realized where the real war was being fought.

The money in my Barclay account, slowly accumulated over the years, would not last more than six months. I needed a job, a place to live, a Canadian driver's license. Without any work history, any job I could get was not going to be very impressive. Restaurant work, maybe. Still, it was better than imprisonment in the United States for terrorism. An odd sort of terrorism: destroying toxins that killed people and animals.

It was possible that DAS, or anybody else, would never even detect the virus Joe had set loose in the world. *P-nitzschia* would just cease producing domoic acid because things mutated. Evolution at work.

My life, too, evolved. I found work at a low-rent diner. The work was hard on my middle-aged feet, but the owner wasn't very particular, or very often present. I drank a lot of coffee to get through my shift. The wages covered my room in a boardinghouse, the food I didn't eat at the diner, and not much else. Not wanting to touch the money in my Barclay account, I put off buying a phone. I made plans for the future, for after enough time had passed that I could feel secure that no one was looking for me. I would join an activist organization, although probably not one concerned with GMOs; that was closed to me now.

But other causes mattered, too. I could still have a genuine life.

A few weeks later, as I sat sipping coffee in an empty booth, waiting for the old couple in the corner to finish their pie, Jake maneuvered through the door in a powerchair.

I knocked over my coffee cup, righted it, sopped at the mess with ineffectual napkins while Jake maneuvered himself up to the table. "Hello, Renata. Love the hair."

I had dyed my hair what the box promised was "Autumn Auburn," and it was a streaky, straw-dry, chemical disaster. I said, "What are you doing here?"

He lowered his sunglasses enough to peer at me over the top, then put them back on. He wore a slouchy fisherman's hat, a cheap windbreaker, baggy pants. On the huge cast on his leg was written BUDWISER, misspelled, in red magic marker. He was unrecognizable, except by me. I would always recognize Jake.

He said, "I got your message."

"You weren't supposed to get my new name and location!"

He shrugged. "I guess somebody thought I should have it."

"But . . . how did you . . ."

"I borrowed Gina's plane, then took three different drivies."

"You must have been recognized at the airport!"

"Of course. But did you not just hear me say that in Canada I took three different drivies? It was a bitch to get in and out of them with this chair. It folds up, but I don't." He began fumbling in a messenger bag.

"Jake," I said in a different tone, "are you . . . will you be all right?"

"Yes. Eventually. Everything is healing. Here, I came to bring you this." He slid a manila envelope across the table.

It held three items. A plane ticket, an index card with an address, and yet another passport. The plane ticket was for next week, first class from Victoria, Canada, to Owen Roberts International Airport, George Town, Grand Cayman Island. The street address was on Grand Cayman. On the passport, the name under my own picture was the same as that on the plane ticket, Julie Jane Tolliver.

"Julie Jane" was what we'd planned to name Ian if he'd been a girl.

I felt my eyes prickle. "How . . ."

"That's what took me so long to get here, along with healing enough that I could get on a plane. With apologies to Flannery O'Connor, a good forger is hard to find. Well, maybe not that hard, but I wanted one that Morgan trusted completely.

I didn't know how solid your fake 'Ellen Tompkins' ID is."

"Morgan knows?"

"Morgan always knows everything. Well, not everything. That address is a beach house that belongs to him. Okay, it now belongs to me, through several shell corporations. That was the other thing that took time. It turns out you can't set up property transfers through nonexistent entities all that fast. Renata, what exactly happened?"

I made a quick decision. I told him but only in vague terms. A secret organization to aid the development, testing, and public opinion of GMO crops. A GMO virus launched into a Northwest Blob to prevent *P-nitzschia* from producing the domoic acid that had killed Ian. Jake listened, his face under the superb control of a gifted actor. But his voice was thick when he finally said, "Then you don't know."

"Know what?"

"What's happening online, and starting to happen offline."

I shook my head. "I have no internet access, and after waitressing all day, I just fall into bed."

"You're too old for this job, Renata."

"Jake Sanderson, always the charmer."

"Get a good phone for Julie Jane and check it out. There's a lot of cash in her account. A very lot." Abruptly his voice turned curt. "I have to go."

"Jake, I appreciate this, but I'm not going to the Caymans. I'm staying here. I can take care of myself."

"Christ, do you think I ever doubted it? You took care of Ian, of me, of as much of the fucked-up world as would let you. You are among the strongest people I know, or maybe just the most stubborn. You faced Ian's death and your grief instead of manically evading it like I—" He couldn't go on.

I reached across the table to take his hand. He let me.

I said, "Julie Jane would be my fourth identity. I might as well be an actor."

Jake gave a shaky laugh before he regained himself. "You don't have to go to the Caymans if you don't want to. But the offer is there, and the plane ticket is good for a year if you give them some notice. I can't visit you there, I'd be recognized."

"Of course you would."

"And there's Gina."

"Yes."

"There are good causes in the Bahamas, too, you know. You wouldn't have to live a pointless life. Lots of good causes."

"Thank you, Jake. I mean it."

"Bye, Renata."

But even as he powered his chair to the door, I

knew I'd see him again, sometime, even if it took a few years. I *felt* it, strong as a healthy heart. I knew that with every single fiber of the bond that held us together. I knew something else, too. Our lives might never mesh well, but I had never, not even in the beginning at Yale, loved him as much as I did in that moment.

It isn't the past that creates the future. It's how you interpret the past.

I finished my shift, left the restaurant, and bought a tablet. The rest of the day and night, I spent in cyberspace.

I had talked to April as little as possible. I should have done so more often. But I hadn't realized, along with everything else I'd been so smugly naïve about, how real wars were now fought. Not with bullets or raids, but with pixels.

Not the cautious, don't-break-the-law posts that the Org had put up before. Those had been water drops; this was a tsunami, trillions of pixels, prepared to be unleashed the moment Joe had launched the virus-scattering missiles.

Videos and statistics about how agribusinesses had poisoned and depleted the soil, created dust bowls, led to monocultures, caused water pollution. Statistics seldom change minds, but images can. Hundreds of different videos, including those of dying sea lions, otters, even whales. The videos were well written and produced and gut-wrenching, the science explained clearly and accurately.

Posts and whole websites about the mistaken ideas of ecoterrorists: "People twist scientific knowledge to reinforce beliefs that are supported not by science but only by their own worldviews."

More videos showing how other GMOs could feed the world. How they hadn't done so because of the use that agribusinesses had put them to: profits for corporations instead of plentiful local food for those in need. "Hunger should not be merely a business opportunity!" How the backlash after the Catastrophe had caused famine and death.

Videos simply and clearly explaining the difference between controlling insects with GMOs that could tolerate sprayed chemicals, which degraded soil and accumulated in human bodies, and GMOs that created disease resistance, so that pesticides and fungicides became mostly unnecessary.

The most care had been lavished on how the genetic engineering of Klenbar, the biopharmed drug that had caused the Catastrophe, differed from what could be done now. The old ways were not the new genetic engineering of possible modified crops. A hammer, after all, can be used to break windows or to build a house. Responsible use of tools was the key.

Millions of posts—at least, it seemed like millions—urged action. Protests, marches, flash mobs, petitions—all the old techniques of civil rebellion. These, the news links reported breathlessly, were just beginning, not many yet and not thousands strong—but they were beginning.

Was all this from the Org? Or had we been working in conjunction with other groups with aligned interests? Who? And who had paid for it all? This campaign represented more resources, more vastly distributed, than I had known the Org possessed. The inescapable conclusion was that we had powerful allies.

Would all this really sway public opinion in favor of crop GMOs? Enough to make a difference? I didn't know.

But seeds had been planted, and the harvest of changed perceptions might grow.

2033: GRAND CAYMAN

THE JUMBO PLANE lifted off and rose through high, thin clouds. I watched Victoria, my residence for eight months but never my home, dwindle beneath me. A beautiful city, but not my city.

Neither was George Town. But, I would be on Grand Cayman Island for only a month, depending on how everything went. Grand Cayman would be sweltering in late July, but I would not be outdoors much.

"All internet devices may now be turned on," the flight-attendant bot said as it rolled down the aisle. Only first class got human attendants, and I was not flying first class. I needed nearly all the money I had for the George Town activity.

Thinking of it as "activity," instead of what it was, made it seem less momentous, and less risky. The games we play on our own minds.

The woman in the seat next to me was already

asleep, or medicated. She snored softly. Across the aisle, a preteen boy in headphones and V-R glasses gestured frantically at something he could see and I could not. His flailing arm hit the shoulder of the man next to him, who looked resigned. I unfolded my tablet for my now-obsessive check on the news.

You never know how any war is going until it's over, and sometimes not until long after that. All you know for sure in the chaos of battle is the fate of individual soldiers. Over the past months, there had been a lot of battles.

More Org stations had been identified and prosecuted by DAS. Those convicted of terrorism included Kyle, April, Jonas, and Tom, the hapless recruit who never had time to actually do anything before he was arrested for not doing it.

Louis Weinberg, eight months after the raid on his carrot station, was still in prison. He refused to enter a plea, determined to use the firestorm of publicity to push the scientific crusade he believed in. Jean and Miguel were still out on bail, awaiting trials that would involve massive discovery efforts and expert witnesses on both sides, and would generate even more publicity than the Org's online war already had.

I never found on the internet anything at all about Joe Peck. That led me to suspect that DAS never identified him, and to hope that he was back with the Quinault Nation, working for NOAA now that funding has been restored.

I didn't know where Dylan was, although I suspected that Jake knew. Five times in eight months, I received letters addressed to Julie Jane Tolliver and postmarked from cities other than Los Angeles. The letters were signed "Tartuffe." They said nothing that couldn't be read by any agency that intercepted them, but in the quotes and reminiscences and obscure allusions, I read undertones of longing. Or maybe that was only my own longing. Online celebrity sites said that Jake and Gina were on the verge of breaking up, but anybody who would trust online celebrity sites would believe in leprechauns, elves, and the wholesomeness of high-fructose corn syrup made from corn drenched with glyphosate.

I did trust the internet sites reporting judicial outcomes. Lisa Anderson's attackers were, all three, in prison for a long, long time.

Who was winning the GMO war? I still didn't know. Both sides were expending stupendous resources to convince the public. But if the eventual outcome wasn't clear, individual battles still had winners and losers.

In New York state, a farmer defiantly and openly planted a crop of GMO onions that fixed nitrogen from the air and so needed no fertilizer, a distinct economic advantage. The crop was torched by ecoterrorists. The farmer sued the group, a case that is getting a lot of attention, and a larger proportion of that attention than I would have expected is on the farmer's side.

In Louisiana, a child wrote to the president that fish were dying in her lake and could the president do something about this? She heard that some "new little animals, too little to see" could fix that. The parents recorded her reading her letter and put it on the internet, a move that would have gone nowhere except that a lunatic state senator declared that the child was an actor and her plea was fake. The child, in tears, made another video. The whole thing went viral, and the mayor of the city declared the child to be a real child. TV and Link comedians seized on this. The senator then made a really stupid mistake: he declared that the mayor, too, was an actor and the whole thing was a left-wing conspiracy. A blight of derision descended over all media—but the GMO bacteria that could clean up oil slicks gained a lot of champions.

A congresswoman in Massachusetts boldly introduced a bill to repeal the Agricultural Security Act.

More farmers planted GMO crops as they realized the economic benefits.

More municipalities risked the oil- or plastic- or garbage-eating GMOs in their waters.

A controversial rock concert in favor of GMOs, Let Us Feed the World, was organized in Los Angeles. I suspected that, way behind the scenes, Jake had something to do with that.

But it's money, not rock music, that powers the world. The whole pro-GMO movement received a huge boost from an unexpected ally: employment.

Under the old agribusinesses, two percent of the population had been engaged in farm work. The new farms were smaller, organic, and genemod—once people realized those two were not exclusive of each other—and they needed more workers. So did the new factories creating specialized bots for the weeding that replaced chemical spraying, the bots for smaller-scale tending and harvesting. It was amazing to me how fast things could be invented and brought to market if that market looked lucrative enough.

More genemod crops appeared in more states, made available by either the Org or some other organization like it. Scientific papers and popular journalism alike were full of them. The most unexpected was intermediate wheatgrass. I knew it had taken hold when I saw recipes appearing for "wheatgrass bread" not just online but in one of the cooking magazines next to a checkout bot. I just hope intermediate wheatgrass bread tastes better than teff pudding.

But what I've followed most closely in my Canadian exile hasn't yet reached the notice of the scientific community, because you can't prove a negative. This summer's algae blooms along the west coast of the United States and Canada have produced no domoic acid. Zip. Zilch. None.

The boy across the aisle flung out an arm so violently that it hit me in the face. His father ripped off the kid's headphones and said, "Robbie!"

"Oh, sorry," Robbie said to me, just before the service bot rolled between us. It said in its carefully calibrated voice, inflected but not human, "What beverage can I get for you, ma'am?"

"Coffee. Cream, no sugar." And to Robbie, "That's okay. Are you winning?"

"Yeah!"

"Go get 'em, Ian."

He frowned. "I'm not Ian, I'm Robert."

"I know."

Puzzled, he shrugged and put his headphones back on.

I went back to my tablet. GMO research and field trials in Africa, Asia, South America. Some of those may find their way to the United States. It will take time, but maybe as the political climate changes along with the global climate, we can still save the world from famine. One carrot at a time.

I want to help. In Victoria, I'd done volunteer work for important causes, but none that mattered to me as much as GMOs. I want to belong again in my own county, working for something I am passionate about. In the Caymans, plastic surgery, like banking, is discreet. Really discreet, even when it's so total that it includes eye replacement, fingerprint replacement, facial realignment—everything necessary to deceive ever-more-sophisticated border security. As long as you have the money, you can start over as somebody else. If I get halfway through the operations to turn me into my fifth identity and I need even more money, I know that Jake will give it to me. However, he will find out about my procedures only when it's either too late to stop them or he gets a death notice as next of kin.

There is a medical risk.

There is a legal risk; a federal arrest warrant is out for Renata Black, aka Renata Sanderson, aka Caroline Denton.

There is a risk that no GMO activist group will take me again.

Let's find out.

Nancy Kress is the best-selling author of more than thirty science fiction and fantasy novels and novellas, including *Beggars in Spain*, *Probability Space*, and *Steal Across the Sky*. To date, she has also published more than ten short story collections and three nonfiction books for *Writer's Digest* on the fundamentals of writing.

Kress is a six-time Nebula Award winner, including two consecutive awards for her novellas *After the Fall, Before the Fall, During the Fall* and *Yesterday's Kin*. She is also the recipient of the Sturgeon and Campbell awards, as well as two Hugo awards. Her fiction has been translated into nearly two dozen languages, including Klingon. Kress teaches writing at workshops, including Clarion West and Taos Toolbox, as well as at the University of Leipzig in Germany, as a guest professor.

Kress lives in Seattle, Washington, with her husband, the author Jack Skillingstead.